W9-BLT-259

POISON *in the* COLONY
JAMES TOWN
1622

Also by ELISA CARBONE

Blood on the River: James Town 1607

Corey's Story

Diana's White House Garden

Heroes of the Surf

Jump

Last Dance on Holladay Street

Many Windows: Six Kids, Five Faiths, One Community
(Co-written with Rukhsana Khan and Uma Krishnaswami)

Night Running

The Pack

Sarah and the Naked Truth

Starting School with an Enemy

Stealing Freedom

Storm Warriors

POISON
in the COLONY

JAMES TOWN 1622

ELISA CARBONE

VIKING

VIKING

An imprint of Penguin Random House LLC

375 Hudson Street

New York, New York 10014

First published in the United States of America by Viking,
an imprint of Penguin Random House LLC, 2019

LIBRARY OF CONGRESS CATALOGING-IN-PUBLICATION DATA IS AVAILABLE.
ISBN 9780425291832

Printed in U.S.A.
Book design by Nancy Brennan
Set in Janson

1   3   5   7   9   10   8   6   4   2

For Emma and Alex,
the next generation of adventurers

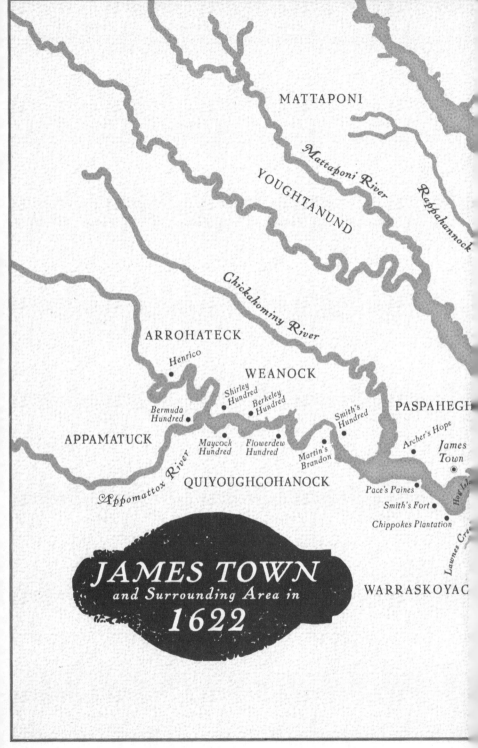

MATTAPONI

Mattaponi River

Rappahannock

YOUGHTANUND

Chickahominy River

ARROHATECK

Henrico

WEANOCK

PASPAHEGH

Shirley
Hundred

Berkeley
Hundred

Smith's
Hundred

Bermuda
Hundred

Archer's Hope

James
Town

APPAMATUCK

Maycock
Hundred

Flowerdew
Hundred

Martin's
Brandon

Hog Isla

QUIYOUGHCOHANOCK

Pace's Paines

Smith's Fort

Appomattox River

Chippokes Plantation

Lawnes Cree

JAMES TOWN
and Surrounding Area in
1622

WARRASKOYAC

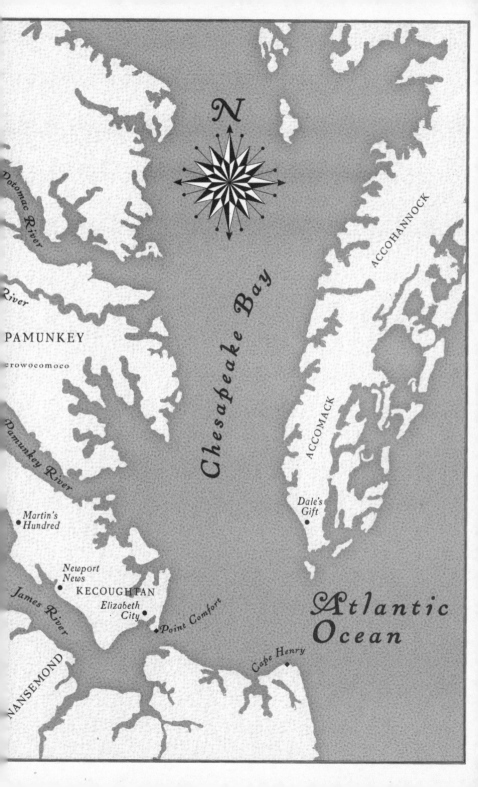

Prologue

———

I AM DIFFERENT.

That is what Samuel says, and I believe he is right.

I was the first one born into the colony. I was the only child to survive the Starving Time. But those things are not what make me different.

It is the knowing that makes me different.

1

MEMORIES

One

IT IS NIGHT. I am sound asleep until Samuel lifts me up from bed. I am small, only three and a half years old. My feet dangle to his knees as he carries me out into the night.

"Where we going?" I ask sleepily.

"Shhh," he whispers, and swings his long strides through the sleeping fort. I trust him. He has always been like a brother to me, a part of our family, as he has no other family. I know that he saved my life and my mother's life when I was a tiny baby.

"I need you to use your knowing," he says to me.

I rest my head against his shoulder and nod. I will do as he asks. I will use the knowing for him, and never tell another living soul about it, as Samuel has warned me not to.

A cat scurries out of our way. An owl calls out her eerie "*Who? Who? Who?*"

"They have kidnapped Matoaka," he says. "They took her away from her family and hid her here. I want you to tell me where she is."

He has stopped walking now. We are at the center of the fort, near the huge cook pot. I straighten up to look into his eyes. "Why?" I ask. "Why did they take her away?" It feels like a very bad thing has happened. If I find her for Samuel, will I undo the bad thing?

Samuel begins to try to explain it all to me: how Captain Argall is holding her for ransom, to get her father, Chief Powhatan, to send us back prisoners and guns. But it is too hard for me to understand, and I am already looking for Matoaka, searching with my mind. I feel each cottage in the fort, the sleeping babies, their dozing mothers and snoring fathers. I close my eyes—the knowing works better that way—and breathe in. I smell urine from full chamber pots, potatoes rotting in storage, lard from the soap-making kettle.

I try to remember Matoaka. Samuel took me to meet her only once, in the Patawomeck village. I played with her little baby boy and she gave me a string of white shells to wear as a necklace. I try to remember the feel of her, her straight, proud back, her sparkling dark eyes and long black hair, her laughter as she and Samuel shared stories about when they were children, told half in English and half in Algonquian. Her husband, Kocoum, a strong young man with gentle hands, patted me on the head and said, "*Netoppew.*" Samuel said it meant "friend."

I take the feeling of her and send my thoughts out to search. *Matoaka, where are you?*

A breeze lifts the dust and makes me cough. And it comes to me—like the *ping* when the blacksmith hits the anvil just right, or one loud clear note played on a flute. I know where she is.

I wriggle down from Samuel's arms and pull him past the cook pot, between the chicken coop and the barn, past the church, to the reverend's cottage.

"Here." I lay my hands against the wattle and daub of the cottage. "She is here."

Samuel scowls and grumbles something about them hiding their "treachery" behind "piety," words I won't understand until I am older. Then he drops to his knees and sets to work, widening a hole in the wattle and daub already started by the rats. He pulls off chunks until the opening is as big as his fist. Then he leans in and whispers loudly.

"Matoaka," he says, using the name only her family and close friends use. "It's us, Samuel and Ginny. We've come to get you free."

We hear the soft padding of bare feet. I push Samuel out of the way. I want to touch Matoaka, to give her some comfort. I reach my hand inside and feel her cold, shaky hand grasp mine. The knowing comes over me with terrible force, making clear what her fate will be.

Tears run down my cheeks. I pull my hand away.

Samuel puts his mouth to the opening. He whispers, telling her how what they've done is wrong, how we're going to get her out of here.

But I know he is powerless. And I know that Matoaka, or Pocahontas as most people call her, will never see her husband and small son again. She will remain a kidnapped prisoner for a very long time.

Two

IT IS EARLY springtime. Outside the open window, the trees wear their lacy new green, and the air is alive with insect sounds. I am four and a half years old. Inside our cottage, my mother is stirring a pot of bubbling cornmeal porridge over the fire—our midday meal. I am standing on a chair, doing my best to pound corn into meal with our large mortar and pestle. My father arrives from working in the fields.

"Ah, my girls are cooking together, I see," he says. He stands behind my mother and wraps his arms around her. His hands come to rest on her slightly bulging belly. I glance at my parents and am surprised to realize what I hadn't noticed before. I flash them a huge smile.

I want to say, *Oh! A new baby is coming!* But I can't let on that I know, and they obviously think it is too early to tell me.

I just keep pounding corn and smiling.

. . .

Pocahontas has been living in Henrico, a new outer plantation far from James Town fort. We receive reports—mostly gossip—as to her well-being.

She is happy. She is angry. She wants to stay with us. She wants to go home. She wears her new English clothing like a princess. She goes barefoot like a commoner under her long dresses. She reads the Bible. Reverend Whitaker has converted her to Christianity and her new Christian name is Rebecca. She will always believe, in her heart, in those heathen gods of theirs: Okeus, Ahone, the Great Spirit.

There is controversy over the ransom. Some say her father has paid some of it but refuses to pay all of what Captain Argall and Governor Dale demand. Others say that her father keeps paying all that they ask, but it is never enough; they always ask for more because they have no intention of allowing her to go home. Some say she is angry at her father. Others say she is furious at Governor Dale and Captain Argall.

The gossip continues: Rebecca is in love with John Rolfe. No, she is not in love, she misses her husband. Her marriage to Kocoum doesn't count because it was not in a church. John Rolfe wants to marry her, and Governor Dale has given his consent.

This last piece of gossip at least, about her marriage to John Rolfe, turns out to be true. A wedding is planned to take place at the church in James Town fort on April 5.

The day dawns warm and sunny. Reverend Buck wears his Sunday black suit. Everyone in the fort wears their finest clothing. For the gentlemen and their wives and children, this means ruffles and starched collars, velvet, lace, and shined shoes. For me and my mother, it means newly washed and mended dresses and clean feet. For my father and Samuel, clean shirts. The Indians come, too: Pocahontas's sister, Mattachanna, and her aunts and uncles, all with their beautiful feathers and necklaces of copper, shells, and beads.

There is a hush, as though if someone says the wrong thing, this magical moment will dissolve—this moment of love and union between our two peoples. We are all tired of the fighting and bloodshed. We want this wedding to bring us peace.

The "better sort" take their seats in the pews, and we stand at the back of the church with the other commoners. I can barely see Mr. Rolfe at the altar with Reverend Buck, waiting for his bride.

Suddenly everyone is on their feet, turning toward us. No, not toward us, toward *her*.

Her black hair is pulled back, her skin dark against the scarlet of her mantle. She is accompanied by her uncle Opitchapam, who will give her away. She carries a bouquet of rosemary and wears a necklace of pearls, a gift from her father. She walks slowly, her face as unreadable as a blank stone.

I desperately want to know what she is thinking and feeling. Is she happy to be marrying John Rolfe? Is she still grief stricken that she can't go home to Kocoum and her young son? I know I only have to touch her, and the knowing will reveal at least some of her feelings to me.

I reach out and brush her hand as she walks by. She doesn't even notice, but I have what I want: the blank stone becomes alive. She is determined, hopeful, nervous, interested, ready for the next step.

Good, I think, *she is making the best of what life has given her.*

I nearly doze off during Reverend Buck's long sermon. But when the wedding is over, when John Rolfe and Rebecca have been pronounced "husband and wife," I am wide-awake. There is joy ruffling through the crowd as we file out of the church. Joy and hope.

Men shake Mr. Rolfe's hand and congratulate him. Rebecca's sister and relatives gather around her. When I see Samuel walking toward Rebecca, I trot after him. He wishes her well and grasps her shoulders as if he could put strength into them—strength she will need, as the peace of two kingdoms rests on those shoulders.

I tug on Rebecca's hand so that she'll notice me. She looks down and I can see that she doesn't recognize me.

"Matoaka," I say. I can't think of anything else to say.

She bends down and takes my face in her palms.

"Ginny?" she asks in amazement. "You're such a big girl now!"

I grin. Then, through her hands, a memory comes to me, almost as if it is my own: a day in her village, her baby son on her lap, her loving husband, Kocoum, nearby. Her eyes fill with tears.

"I'm so sorry," I whisper.

But it startles her, and I realize I have said a very stupid thing on her wedding day. "Um, I mean, be happy. Be happy *now*," I say.

She blinks, quickly wipes tears from her cheeks, and laughs. "Yes, Ginny," she says. "Thank you."

Three

———

AUGUST 1614

IT IS THE flush of full summer. Soon I will be five years old. My mother's belly is tight and round, and my father has announced proudly to me that before long I will have a baby brother. I know the child is a girl, but I don't tell him.

Right after breakfast, Samuel arrives at our cottage. "Ready?" he asks my mother.

She is combing the knots out of my dark brown curls and I am wincing with each pull. I'm glad Samuel has arrived to save me from this hair combing.

"Yes," Mum says. She ties back my hair, knots and all, and puts my bonnet on securely. "Virginia, come. Let's see what you have learned."

We set off for the meadow and the forest. My mother knew herbs and healing in England, taught by her mother, and Samuel learned about the herbs here in the New World from the natives when he lived in the Warraskoyack village. Some of the herbs here are the same as in England, but many are not. Samuel taught the new ones to my mother, and they have both been teaching me.

There is a din of crickets and cicadas, the sweet music of late summer. A crow watches from a tree, squawking out his comments, *"Caw! Caw!"*

I am still too young to leave the fort on my own, and so this foray into the wild is a rare adventure. I am ecstatic. The forest is where the trees and plants, even the rocks and dirt, let me know they are alive with the same life and joy that is in me. At the edge of the wood I run to a tree and lay my palms against the trunk. I feel the life pulsing under the bark. Then I lean in close. "Hello," I whisper. I bound away, knowing I won't exactly hear a "hello" back.

I find a big rock and sit down on it. There is life here, too, though it is so quiet I have to sit very still to feel it. "How are you today?" I ask softly. I already know the answer. If the rock could speak, it would say, "Happy."

Next, I am on to the ferns, holding their fronds, feeling the life of water and sun running through them.

"Look at her," I hear my mother say to Samuel. "Such a strange child."

I snatch my hands away from the ferns. Quickly, I pick up a stick and look for some dirt to dig in. That is what other children would do.

"She's just having fun being out of the fort," Samuel tells my mother.

"Virginia, come here," my mother says. "Let's see what you remember."

I am very happy to be tested. For this, I am allowed to touch the plants without my mother worrying that I am acting strange. She thinks I am remembering what she has taught me on other visits to the meadow and forest, and some of it I do remember, but it is even easier to listen to each plant for the correct answer.

I find a slippery elm tree. I recite how the inner bark can be made into a poultice to heal wounds, or taken as a medicine for sore throats. Then, at the forest's edge, I find black raspberry—the leaves to speed childbirth, and the roots to treat the summer flux. Next, I find the velvet-soft leaves of mullein, for coughs and earaches. I point to the stinging nettles. These I do not touch. "For skin problems," I say, but since touching them *causes* skin problems, I think that staying away from them might be the best remedy of all. I find purple coneflower in full bloom. "It's good for infections and fevers," I say.

Mum claps her hands. "Good girl," she says.

"It's also good for snakebites," I say, gently stroking the large delicate petals.

Mum shakes her head. "No, that is not correct."

I drop my hands to my sides. The knowing is clear. This flower can help get rid of the poison of a snakebite. "We should try it," I say very softly.

Mum gives Samuel a worried glance. He simply shrugs.

"All right, you did quite well," Mum says.

"Soon the colonists will come to you for healing instead of your mum," Samuel teases.

Mum gives me scissors so that I can help cut and gather the plants. As we work, I eavesdrop. Samuel tells my mother the news he has heard as he has traveled to other plantations and to Indian villages.

"Since the wedding in April, there's been no fighting. Not a single arrow or musket has been fired," Samuel says. "People are calling it 'The Peace of Pocahontas.'"

"Thanks be to God," my mother says.

"Have you heard, Governor Dale tried to take another wife?" Samuel asks.

"That man has no shame," Mum says.

Samuel continues. "He sent a messenger to Chief Powhatan to ask for the hand of his eleven-year-old daughter in marriage."

Mum raises her eyebrows. "And did Lady Dale send word from England that this would be fine with her?"

Samuel laughs. "The chief said no, of course. He told the messenger the girl was in a village three days' walk away. He will keep her well protected, I'm sure."

"Good," my mother says. "Governor Dale is an evil man, with his martial law and whippings and hangings. I wish the Company would send back Captain Smith and send Governor Dale home to England with his tail between his legs."

Mum and Samuel continue their gossip and gathering, and I am free to play in the magic of the forest.

• • •

It is a day without breezes, and mosquitoes buzz around our heads even inside the cottage. Mum and I work together to hang herbs to dry. I tie the strings and she lifts the bunches to hang them on nails set in the rafters.

There is a knock at the door. It is a gentleman. Mum gives him a curious look. The gentlemen and nobles normally go to the doctor for their healing, while the common folk come to my mother or Jane Wright, the left-handed midwife.

The gentleman is distraught, his face twisted in fear. It is his wife who is ill—very ill. The doctor has already seen her and given her medicine, but she has not improved. Can my mother help? He is afraid she is dying.

Mum asks the man what his wife is feeling, and as he speaks, she chooses which plants to bring. "These will help," she says.

I go with her and we follow the man to his cottage. Mum has me wait outside. There is a boy, a little older than I, sitting in the dirt in front of the cottage. He is sullen, as fearful as his father. He glares at me. It is the first time I've seen this boy.

• • •

The second time I see the boy, and his father, is a few days later. It is evening. The gentleman pounds on our door and when my father opens it, he grabs my da by his shirt collar.

"She said she could help!" he cries. "I should have known better than to come to the likes of her. The doctor had given her medicine. She would have gotten better if that woman"—he points a long, accusing finger at my mother—"hadn't laid her cursed hands on her."

My da is trying to close the door on him. The boy is behind his father, staring at me with a hateful look.

"I will make a report," the man shouts. Then he narrows his eyes and lowers his voice. "I know who your mother was, Mrs. Laydon." He turns, grabs his son by the arm, and drags him away.

Mum collapses into a chair and hangs her head into her hands. "I should have known better than to try to heal a gentleman's wife," she says miserably.

"You could not turn him away," Da says. He lays a hand on her shoulder.

I am afraid to ask any questions.

• • •

My mother and Jane Wright work together in our cottage. It is night, and the candles flicker over their needles as they sew. They, and other women as well, have been assigned to make shirts for the servants of the colony. I am seated at the table with them, practicing my stitches with my own piece of cloth, needle, and thread. Now that I am almost five, it is time I learned to sew. When I hear my mother yelp, I look up.

"It broke again," she says. There is a hint of desperation in her voice. "The thread is bad. We won't have nearly enough to finish."

"Mum, use mine." I hold my little bit of thread out to her.

She shakes her head. She and Jane are looking at each other.

"A trap?" Mum asks Jane.

Jane frowns. She picks at the woven cloth at the bottom of the shirt she is working on and it begins to unravel. The thread that comes free is strong and good. "A trap we might be able to avoid," she says.

They work quickly, unraveling the bottoms of the shirts, using the good thread to finish their stitching. They have no choice. There is no other thread.

I feel their panic and I don't understand it. I try to rest my cheek against my mother's arm, but she shrugs me off. I go to bed while they are still working.

Four

———

THERE IS A trial. Under Governor Dale's martial law, there is no hearing, no jury, just the governor's decision. And Governor Dale pronounces my mother and Jane Wright guilty of stealing thread from the Company. The shirts they made were shorter than those made by the other women—the women who were given good thread to work with.

Their punishment? A brutal whipping.

My father carries my mother home. He is weeping and cursing. He lays her in bed. She is silent.

I heat water on the fire and, with clean rags, bathe my mother's cut and bloody back. She lies on her side, flinching as I do my work. Every few minutes her breathing becomes ragged, until finally she cries out, "Get Jane!"

I look to my father. Surely Jane is in her bed as well. My father nods to me, and I go.

I find Jane sitting in her cottage, leaning onto the table, the top of her dress down, her head hanging. Her husband stands behind her, washing her wounds. She moans quietly. Her back is just as cut and bloody as my mother's. I am filled with hatred for Governor Dale.

"My mother is asking for you," I say, barely above a whisper.

"Oh please, no," Jane says. She tries to stand but groans in pain.

"You can't go," her husband says, and helps her to sit back down.

"I cannot leave her to die," Jane says, her voice strong. "Robert, lay that rag on my back for a bandage and help me on with my dress." She winces as Robert does as she says.

She picks up her bag—the bag she brings with her to heal the sick and to deliver babies—and I follow her out the door.

At home my mother is on her feet, her arm draped over my father's shoulders. My father's eyes are wild.

"She's—it's not time!" he blurts out.

"I know, John," Jane says. Her voice is the one calm thing in the room. "Virginia, you have hot water on the fire? Good. Fill a bowl with it for me and bring me an empty bowl as well." She begins to take things out of her bag: a packet of herbs, scissors, a small blanket.

I am confused, but I set to work, finding bowls and hot water. My mother slumps onto the bed and sits for a moment. Then she groans and stands again, clinging to my father.

"You're going to be all right, Ann," Jane says. "I will make sure of it."

My mother nods at her friend. Sweat drenches her face. Her eyes have the look of a trapped animal. She cries out. Jane crouches in front of her.

I take small steps, carefully carrying the bowl of hot water to Jane. When I reach her, what I see in her hands does not make sense. It is a baby that is impossibly small, hardly bigger than Jane's hand, with the cord still attached to its belly. I blink, not believing. The baby is not breathing or moving. With a rush, I realize this is my baby sister. Born too early. Much too early.

My mother sobs. "He is a murderer!" she cries.

My father smooths her hair, tries to comfort her.

I feel dizzy. I stumble out of the cottage. It is quiet and dark and somehow peaceful outside. Fireflies glitter their lights on and off. In the sky overhead, the stars shine, unchanging. I look up into the night. "Why did Governor Dale do that?" I whisper. "Why did he set a trap for Mum and Jane? Why did he give them bad thread?"

I close my eyes, hoping that my prayer and the knowing will work together to give me an answer. But my mind is as empty as the darkness between the stars.

• • •

Governor Dale struts through the fort, his deputy at his side. His starched collar holds his head up high as though he is looking down on all of us. In my imagination, I pull an arrow from the quiver on my back and string it tight to my bow. I let it fly. It strikes him in the heart.

A voice startles me. "There are daggers in your eyes, Virginia."

It is Jane Wright. She has caught me in my hateful stare. She bends down and puts a hand on my cheek. "Wish for good things, little one, not bad things. Wish for something good for your mother and for the colony."

I look up at her. "I wish for Governor Dale to go back to England." I say it quietly, so no one else will hear me.

She smiles and leans in to whisper, "That is a good wish for the colony."

Five

I AM SIX and a half years old. I have been wishing for good things, and some of them have appeared.

Rebecca and John Rolfe have a baby boy. They have named him Thomas, and we hear that he is walking already. I wished for happiness for Matoaka, and I know that this child must be bringing her joy.

I have a new baby sister, Alice. Maybe I should have been more specific and told God to send me a brother to please my father even more, but my wishes were for my mother to be healed and joyful again, and for a healthy baby. Alice is still very small. She grasps my finger tightly and kicks her legs. She will have to be strong to survive.

The gentleman who blamed my mother for his wife's death has since died as well, and so he has been no more trouble to us. But his son, whose name is Charles, still lives in James Town, boarding with another gentleman's family. Charles despises me, though about the worst he has done is throw rocks at me, and I am a fast runner, so I can generally avoid being hit.

I have been wishing for a sweetheart for Samuel, as he is now twenty years old and says he is ready to marry. It seems to me every young girl in the colony flirts with him, tall and handsome as he is. But he is interested in none of them. He keeps saying he'll see what the next ship brings in, and the next, and the next. I suppose some wishes take longer than others to come true.

The biggest and best wish of all to come true? A ship arrives. It is the *Treasurer*, captained by Samuel Argall. After many letters of complaint against Governor Dale sent to London, and his time of service to the colony being over, the Company is replacing him with a new governor, Sir George Yeardley. When the *Treasurer* sets sail back to England, Governor Dale will be on it. And I will imagine a long, pointy tail tucked between his legs as he boards that ship to leave us forever.

The *Treasurer* bobs in the water at the docks on a sunny spring day. The new settlers are allowed off first: gentlemen, servants, wives, and children. They walk down the gangplank looking dazed and curious. Did they expect stone buildings or horses and carriages like I've heard they have in England? Are they shocked by the natives who live and work among us, with their dark skin, leather clothing, feathers, and beads? When I see new settlers staring wide-eyed at our settlement, I think about England and how different it must be.

And on this bright, warm day, I wonder if these people are ready for what is in their future. Are they ready for the steamy heat of summer, clouds of mosquitoes, the summer flux that takes the strength, and the lives, of the hardiest men? Are the laborers ready for the grueling work in the tobacco fields? Are they ready for icy wind whistling through the leaky cottages in winter? Are they ready for the hungry months of March and April, when our stores run dangerously low, our stomachs growl day and night, and we watch the horizon for a ship to come with new stores? I know that no one is allowed to send letters back to England telling the truth about how difficult life is here, and so I wonder if the people coming off the ship have any idea what awaits them.

After the passengers have disembarked, men work to unload supplies from the ship: barrels of barley and peas and salt pork, crates of squawking chickens, hogs that snort as they are led down the gangplanks to land. As soon as the ship is unloaded, barrels and crates of things we have been producing are loaded into the hold: pitch, tar, sassafras, clapboard, sturgeon, and tobacco. Lots and lots of tobacco.

John Rolfe was the first to come up with the idea of growing tobacco here to sell in England. The Virginia

Company of London is all for it because they're finally making a profit from James Town. But we have heard that King James thinks that tobacco is horrible stuff and says it is "a custom loathsome to the eye, hateful to the nose, harmful to the brain, and dangerous to the lungs."

The *Treasurer* sits at dock for a few days, and during this time an exciting new rumor begins to spread through James Town: When she sets sail, the *Treasurer* will carry John, Rebecca, and Thomas Rolfe for a visit to England.

I realize the rumor must be true when Rebecca's sister, Mattachanna, and her husband, the priest To-mocomo, come to James Town. They will be going too, along with a group of servants from the Powhatan tribe.

On the day the ship is to set sail, the Rolfe family arrives from Henrico. Rebecca holds little Thomas. He looks so much like her! She smiles and greets Matta-channa and Tomocomo. It seems like everyone in James Town goes out to see the ship off.

There are so many people, all pressing to get close to the travelers, that I don't even try to say goodbye. I stand with my father and mother. Alice sleeps in my mother's arms, despite all the noise and shouting. I watch as Rebecca walks up the gangplank, then turns to take one more look at her homeland. I can't tell if she is happy or sad—she is too far away.

"She's determined to find out if Captain Smith is

alive or dead, you know." It is Samuel, come to join us, talking to my father.

"I hear she'll meet King James himself," my father says.

Samuel laughs. "I should have told her to bring a perfumed handkerchief to hold against her nose when she meets that smelly old fellow."

My father laughs, too. Everyone knows King James believes that bathing causes the plague, and so he only takes a bath once a year.

Rebecca walks the last few steps up the gangplank and onto the ship. She looks back at all of us, the sun on her face. Suddenly the knowing washes over me, dizzying, certain, horrible: she will never return. She will die in England. Soon.

"Oh no!" I cry out.

Samuel, my father, and my mother all turn to me. Samuel is frowning. He must know it is the knowing, and he is reminding me to say nothing.

"What is it, Virginia?" my mother demands. My baby sister has slept through all the other shouting, but my voice has awakened her and she begins to fuss.

"It's . . . it's . . ." I try to think of something to say.

Samuel glares at me. Then he rescues me. "I know, Ginny," he says comfortingly. "I forgot to give her a gift for her journey, too. But she will be back in a year and we can both give her gifts to welcome her." He grabs my hand. "Come on, now, and help me with my mending like you've been promising, before I have to get to the fields."

He pulls me away from my parents, away from the crowd. When I look back, Rebecca has disappeared and I know she must have climbed down into the 'tween deck, where she and the other passengers will spend the voyage.

When we are out of earshot, he stops and faces me. "Is it about Matoaka?" he asks.

I nod and my eyes well up with tears. "She's never coming back," I whisper. "She will die before a year is over."

Samuel clenches his jaw. "They should have let her stay here," he says. "This is where she belongs."

"Did she want to go?" I ask.

"Nothing is her choice, Ginny," he says. "She is still a prisoner in so many ways. Governor Dale says she will go, and so she must go. He wants to show her off—the Indian princess converted to Christianity."

"But . . ." He has not answered my question. "Did she *want* to go?"

Samuel gives me a slight smile. "She says it will be an adventure, and that as long as little Thomas is with her, she will be happy."

I breathe out a sigh. "I hope she sees lots of wonderful things in the time she has left," I say.

As I walk home, I wonder about the knowing. I wonder why sometimes I can choose to use it, through touch or through a sort of inner listening. I wonder why, at other times, it comes like a bird swooping down from the sky, unexpected. And I wonder why Samuel is so adamant that I never tell another living soul about it.

Six

———

I AM SEVEN and a half years old. My mother sends me to the river to dig for mussels, and so I am one of the first to see it: a ship on the horizon. Soon there are calls throughout the fort: "Ship ashore! Ship ashore!"

People come wandering toward the docks. We are all running low on our food stores, and so there are high hopes for what this ship might bring. We are also expecting the return of Captain Argall, who is to take over as governor. Even my mother comes to the docks, with little Alice toddling along, holding her hand.

I go to Alice and scoop her up. "See, it's a ship," I say. "A big boat."

"Ba," says Alice.

"It'll have peas and beans for you to eat. And barley, lots of barley," I tell her.

"Ba," she says.

Suddenly, someone shouts, "It is the *Treasurer*! It must

be John Rolfe and Rebecca and Thomas coming home!"

People begin to chatter with excitement:

"They met the king!"

"They must have been invited to balls and plays and masques."

"I hope she found Captain Smith."

"Ah, the stories we'll hear about their year in England!"

My stomach twists into a knot. I know that when the *Treasurer* lands, it will bring bad news instead of joy.

My mother is staring at me. "Are you not happy to see Rebecca again?" she asks. There is a challenge in her voice, and I know that she is somehow suspicious. But how could she be? I've never said one word about the knowing to anyone but Samuel.

I quickly put on a smile, though it feels as if it reaches only my mouth and not my eyes. "Yes, I am very happy," I say. "We'll hear stories about England." My words catch in my throat and I have to look away. Before the ship's arrival I could still imagine her alive and well. But soon, everyone will know what I have known for a year.

My mother will not let it rest. She takes hold of my face and turns me toward her. There is fear in her eyes. She shakes her head slightly and whispers, "Oh child, no."

My mother and I stand next to each other, among settlers giddy with excitement, grimly awaiting the bad news that we both now expect.

It is worse than even I knew.

Samuel comes to our cottage for supper, and after our meal, he and my father sit talking in hushed voices.

"Mattachanna and Tomocomo say she was perfectly well when she left to have dinner with Captain Argall and her husband. They say she must have been poisoned. She died within hours of coming back from dinner," says Samuel.

My father shakes his head sadly. "And Captain Argall insists it was illness."

"One thing is for certain," Samuel says, "Captain Argall will never be punished if he did murder her with poison at that dinner. His only accusers are not English citizens."

"We may never know the truth," my father says.

Samuel glances over at me, as though the knowing would give me details anytime I ask it. I scowl at him. All I know is that Rebecca is gone, and now there are two motherless boys: her son with Kocoum, living in one of the Indian villages, and little Thomas, left back in England to be raised by John Rolfe's brother.

Samuel lowers his voice and thinks I can't hear. He says to my father, "How long do you think the peace will last with her gone?"

My mother has been agitated and sullen all afternoon. Did she care so much for Rebecca that she is now grieving? She gathers our soiled clothes into a bundle.

"Virginia, come help me with this washing," she says. Then she plops Alice onto my father's lap and leads me out the door.

What a strange time to do laundry, I think, in the evening, when the drying sun is almost down. And my mother loves to gossip with the other women while we wash. At this hour, there won't be anyone else there.

I follow her obediently. When we reach the river, all is quiet except for the spring peepers chirping. I decide to wash Alice's clothes first, as they are the dirtiest. I tie up my skirt and wade into the water. The chill makes me shiver.

Suddenly my mother's hands are upon me, yanking me down, pushing me underwater. I struggle, kick, try to pull her hands away. She pushes harder, her weight holding me under. *Air! Air! Breath!* I dig my fingernails into her hands and claw the skin away. She screams and lets go.

I am up, heaving in a breath, water dripping into my eyes. I see my mother's face: terror. She reaches for me again, pushes me hard. I fall, and she is upon me, holding me under.

A clear, cold thought enters my mind: *She is killing me.* Darkness crowds my vision. I go limp. She pulls me up out of the river and shakes me hard. I cough and sputter.

My mother is sobbing now. I am too exhausted and confused to run from her. Her hands are bleeding where

I clawed them. She reaches out to hold my face in her palms. I flinch, but when she touches me, I feel her love—it has not changed. I feel her love for me, and her fear of something terrible. It is fear that has made her do this to me. She wants me to be just as afraid as she is.

"You must kill it in yourself, Virginia," she says. "Do you understand me? You must kill it, or they will kill you. They will torture you to get a confession—hang you by your thumbs until the pain is so great, you will tell them whatever they want to hear. Then they will strangle you—cut off your air just like when you were under the river, but they will not let go the way I did. When you are dead, they will burn your body and spit on your ashes."

She takes a shivery breath and seems to be staring right through me. In a small voice, she says, "That is what they did to your grandmother."

I shake my head hard. I don't want to hear these terrible things.

My mother continues, "You saw what they did to me and Jane Wright. What was our sin? To know about healing and herbs? That I tried to help that dying gentlewoman? Because Jane delivered a baby who did not survive? That gentleman found out what they did to my mother in England. He decided I must be suspect as well. All it takes is one gentleman or nobleman, or even a yeoman, to cast suspicion, Virginia. And out comes the whip . . . or the strangling cord and the pyre."

"Your mother knew healing and herbs—" I begin. I am afraid to ask what else was the cause of her tortured death. The death of a convicted witch.

Mum nods. "Yes, she was a healer." She looks into my eyes. "And she had the gift of the second sight."

My whole body begins to shake. My mother wraps her arm around me and guides me out of the river. She sits with me on a fallen log and rocks me in her embrace.

"I call it the knowing," I say in a small voice. "That's what Samuel named it."

I feel her body stiffen. "Samuel knows?" she asks.

"Yes," I say. "But no one else. He told me never to tell anyone."

She relaxes. "We must not even tell your father. He is already worried that the second sight will be passed from my mother through me and on to our daughters. That is one of the reasons he is always hoping for a son." She kisses the top of my head. "Kill it in yourself, Virginia. Promise me you will do that?"

"I promise," I say. I don't know how I'll do it, but for her safety and mine, I know I must.

2

POISON

Seven

APRIL 1619

"BERMUDA EASON, THAT is no way to bait a fish-hook!" I snatch the hook and the wiggler from him and stab the wiggler firmly onto the hook.

Bermuda grimaces. His sandy-blond curls stick out from under his cap.

"You're worse than my little sister," I say, and hand the hook back to him. He casts it into the river.

"Mum says I better catch something today," Bermuda mumbles. "Our corn is almost gone."

"Ours too," I say. The natives call March the hungry month, but for us sometimes April is even hungrier as we wait for the first spring ships to arrive with new stores.

We are at our favorite fishing spot at Glass House Point, where the land juts out into the river and the water ripples by, making a swishing sound. There is a lightness to the day. We are officially done with two years of Captain Argall as our governor. He will go back to England on the first supply ship to stand trial for the many accusations by colonists against him. Our new governor once again is Sir George Yeardley, who has always been a fair man.

A great blue heron lands on a rock nearby, then, standing on one leg, looks at us.

"We're not sharing with you," Bermuda tells the bird.

And with that, the heron flies off.

"Want to skip rocks?" Bermuda asks.

"Sure," I say. We can hold our fishing sticks with one hand and throw with the other.

It makes sense that Bermuda and I would be friends. We were both born in the New World when it was first being settled by the English. Bermuda was born on the island he was named after, when his ship was marooned there in 1609. He is a little younger than I, though sometimes he seems a lot younger. Maybe it's true what my mother says whenever I'm too bossy: that I am approaching my teen years faster than other girls my age.

Also, Bermuda and I are both children of commoners but our parents are well respected because they have been here for so long. They are among the group called "the ancients," even though my mother is only twenty-five and my father is in his thirties.

Bermuda sends a flat rock skimming across the water, ending in a staccato of tiny skips. "Ha! Fourteen!" Bermuda grins, proud of himself.

"How could you even count those, they were so fast," I say. But it is clear he has won the contest. I have only been able to get six skips, no matter how perfect a skipping rock I find. It's about the only thing Bermuda does better than I do, which is why he always wants to play.

Suddenly there are rocks plopping into the water—rocks neither Bermuda nor I have thrown. I turn toward the trees to see where they are coming from and one hits me squarely in the forehead.

"Ah!" I cry. There is blood on my hand when I touch my face.

"Charles, get yourself gone!" Bermuda shouts. He aims a large rock and throws it hard.

I see the back of Charles's waistcoat as he scrambles off between the trees.

"That stupid boy," Bermuda says. He peers at my face. "It's not bleeding very much."

"I'll be fine," I say. It feels good to have Bermuda sticking up for me.

"I wish he would figure out it was sickness that killed his mother, not anything your mum did," Bermuda says.

"I wish he'd move to one of the plantations," I say.

Bermuda hands me my fishing stick, which I dropped when I got hit.

"I'll race you home after we catch our fish," I say.

He rolls his eyes. Nobody beats me in footraces, not

even the older children who arrive from Europe.

But we don't race home. We walk back, as the sun dips behind the trees, knowing our mothers will want us for chores, and knowing they will both be disappointed that we didn't catch anything.

As we pass the old glass house, Bermuda insists on looking inside. Sometimes this is where the German and Polish craftsmen come to sit and drink their ale. But there is no one here today. All is quiet, with only the ghosts of the men who worked here when the colony first began and glassmaking was one of the industries.

"Can't you just see it?" Bermuda asks, his voice full of wonder. "A fire in the furnace so hot it melts sand, me running back and forth. 'More wood, Bermuda! More wood, I say,' my boss is yelling at me. 'Blow the bellows, Bermuda. Keep that fire *hot!*'" He pretends to pump a large bellows. "Then, when I'm older, they'll teach me to make the glass. I'll have my long rod, and the melted glass, and I'll blow and blow." He blows on his imaginary rod. "Look! I've made a wine flask."

"Very nice," I say, playing along, seeing his clear green flask in my mind's eye.

Bermuda is quiet, looking around at the dusty glass house, the tattered roof, the cold furnaces, the shards of broken glass on the floor. "They'll start it up again some-day," he says. "I know they will."

"It's been almost ten years since they've tried to make glass," I say. "It didn't work. Why would they try again?"

He huffs at me. "It did work. My da still has a drinking glass that was made here."

"You know what I mean. It didn't make enough money when they sold the glass in England. That's all the Company cares about—profits." Our colony is owned by the Virginia Company of London. Their main mission is to make a profit from James Town for their shareholders and investors, either from something we can find, like the gold they were first hoping for, or from something we can produce here to be sold in England.

Bermuda frowns, and I suddenly feel bad for dashing his dreams. "Maybe someday you can sail to England and become an apprentice to a glassblower there," I suggest.

"No," he says. "I want to do it here."

He marches ahead of me up the hill. I am tempted to continue arguing with him, but for his sake, I decide to keep my mouth shut. When we are almost to the fort, Cecily comes running to meet us.

"Ginny, I've been looking all over for you," she says. She is out of breath. Her blonde hair has strayed in wisps from her bonnet and her cheeks are bright red. She is one of several girls of marriageable age who always want to know where Samuel is, what he has said about them, what color eyes he likes in a girl, and all kinds of other silly questions that I could do without.

"What do you need, Cecily?" I ask, bracing myself for yet another silly question.

"It's Samuel—his leg. He's asking for you. He says he's dying." She blurts it out.

I toss my fishing stick to Bermuda. "Where is he?" I demand.

"At your cottage."

I take off running.

Eight

I HEAR CRIES of pain as soon as I enter the fort. It is Samuel's voice.

I run to our cottage and burst inside. Samuel is on the bed, writhing and shouting. Gathered around him are several of his friends, Reverend Buck, and my mother, who is bathing his leg with a bloody rag.

I drop to my knees beside him. "Samuel, what is it? What happened to you?"

He grasps my hand and squeezes so hard it hurts. "Stingray," he growls through clenched teeth.

"We were fishing. He was wading in shallow water," one of his friends says.

"We pulled the barb out, but the poison was already in him," says another of his friends.

The young men hang their heads and shuffle their feet, looking helpless and guilty, as if they should have been able to do something.

"Ginny." Samuel grimaces as he talks. "I need you to

tell me. Am I going to die?" He lets out another agonized groan.

Reverend Buck looks at me sharply. I see my mother stiffen. How could Samuel be asking me this, when he knows how dangerous it is for me and my family? He must be half crazed, or completely crazed, by the pain. The knowing is trying to nudge me, trying to rise up and answer Samuel's question, even though I have done my best to kill it for two years now—drown it deep in the waters of my mind. I shove it back down, take a deep breath, and answer, "Yes."

Samuel lets out a long cry. "I knew it! Dig my grave. I am ready to lie in it."

Reverend Buck is scowling at me. "How do you know this, Virginia?" he demands.

My mother lets the rag slip into the bowl of bloody water. I'm afraid she might faint.

I stand and straighten my back. "Because we will all die, Reverend. It is the way of things."

My mother breathes out a quick sigh. The reverend's face softens. Samuel groans. "No, Ginny, I mean today." He grunts and tries to raise himself up on one elbow. "Am I going to die *today*?"

I put out my hands, palms up. "How in the world am I supposed to know?"

Samuel flops back down. I run to get my mother's long wooden spoon, the one with the teeth marks on the handle from when she was in labor with Alice. I go to Samuel and place the spoon handle across his mouth. "Here," I say. "Bite on this. It will help with the pain."

Samuel bites down. *There*, I think, *that will shut him up.*

I sit on the bed with Samuel. "You told me the story a hundred times," I say. "About Captain Smith and the stingray."

Samuel nods. Beads of sweat stand out on his forehead.

"When Captain Smith got the barb shot into his leg from his stingray, he thought he would die, right?" I ask.

Samuel lets out a howl and thrashes so hard, he almost kicks my mother.

"Make the water even hotter," my mother says. I go to the fire and bring back the steaming kettle. We know, from others who have been stung, that very hot water is the only thing that helps with the pain.

"Not everyone dies from these stings," Reverend Buck offers.

"Captain Smith *ate* his stingray after he recovered," says my mother. "We've got yours right here, Samuel. We'll cook it up for you. You just get through this, and you can eat it later."

Samuel nods quickly, the spoon bobbling up and down.

I grasp his hand again and squeeze almost as hard as he squeezes me. "Be as strong as Captain Smith," I say.

Nine

___

NOW I HAVE two constant companions. Alice has been my little shadow almost since she could walk. Getting my chores done while she "helps" makes everything twice as hard. But now I also have Samuel.

Samuel is recovering well from the stingray attack. He relished eating the odd-looking creature and shared the meat with us as well. But his leg was so torn up from where they pulled out the barb, it is still too painful for him to work in the fields or tend the cattle.

Others who have been stung died later of infection or gangrene, so Samuel is sticking close to me and my mother, having us check the wound and treat it with herbs. He hobbles over each morning and plops himself down, ready to talk.

On the third day of this, I decide our cottage is too small, too hot, and too smoky for all of us, so I bring my work, and my entourage, outside. My mother leaves to fetch water and to see if there is a ration of eggs for us. I build a fire in our outdoor pit and put our porridge on to cook. I set Alice on the ground with a few kernels of corn and a small mortar and pestle that we normally use for herbs. Then I go to work with the big stone mortar and pestle to grind our corn. Samuel sits on a chair with his leg propped up on a log. He swats at the buzzing flies.

I notice that the bandage, which is supposed to cover the back of his calf, is mostly falling off. I figure it is good for the wound to get some air, so I leave it hanging open.

"Tell me about the prophecy," I say. This is a conversation he always enjoys, talking about the prophecy given to Chief Powhatan by his high priests shortly before the first English ships came to James Town. It has been one year since Chief Powhatan died. Some say he died of grief after he learned that his favorite daughter, Pocahontas, had died in England. His brothers, Opitchapam and Opechancanough, have taken over his position as paramount chiefs over all the tribes.

Samuel tips his head back, letting the sun shine on his face. He begins to recite the prophecy:

"In the time of the first planting of corn, there will come a tribe from the bay of the Chesapeake."

"That was you, the first three ships," I say. "You and

Captain Smith and my father and all the rest. You landed in April, and you were that tribe, because you sailed up the Chesapeake Bay."

Samuel nods. We have recited this together many times, ever since I was small.

I fill in the rest of my part: "And Chief Powhatan had the Chesapeake tribe all killed or captured because he thought *they* were the tribe in the prophecy."

Samuel continues, *"This tribe will build their long-houses on the land of the Powhatan. They will hunt and fish and plant on the land of the Powhatan."*

"That was your settlement, when you built the first cottages in James Town," I say. "Then there were the battles. . . ."

"Yes," says Samuel. *"Three times the Powhatan will rise up against this tribe. The first battle will end and the Powhatan will be victorious."*

"The first battle ended when Captain Smith and Chief Powhatan became countrymen," I say. "Then there was peace." Captain Smith is a hero to me and to many. Samuel says he was very brave and fair.

Samuel goes on, *"But the tribe will grow strong again. The Powhatan will rise up. The second battle will end and the Powhatan will be victorious."*

"That battle started when Captain Smith went back to England and the leaders here went on a rampage against the Indians," I say. "But it's over now. We are at peace."

Samuel swats at a fly. "Yes. The Peace of Pocahontas."

My stomach twists. I hear Samuel's voice in my head, speaking to my father two years ago when Pocahontas died: *How long do you think the peace will last with her gone?*

"We are still at peace, even with Rebecca gone," I say hopefully.

Samuel goes back to reciting. *"But the tribe will grow strong once more. The third battle will be long and filled with bloodshed. By the end of this battle, the Powhatan kingdom will be no more."*

We are silent for a time. This last part has always seemed impossible to me. How could the Powhatan kingdom ever "be no more"? There are so many more of them than there are of us—thousands more. And this is their land, their country. Chief Powhatan, up until he died last April, said he wanted to live at peace with us. And now the new leaders, his brothers, have vowed to keep that peace. Though each individual tribe and town has its own chief, Chief Opechancanough and Chief Opitchapam rule over all the tribes together. If they want peace, then all of the tribes must listen to them.

"Do you think the last part is true?" I ask Samuel. "Maybe the Indian priests made a mistake when they gave the prophecy."

He shrugs. "Maybe they did." He senses my discomfort. "And maybe it will be many years from now before it happens."

I pound the pestle into the grain, letting the rhythm calm me. "I hope we stay at peace for a long time," I say. "Forever."

"We all do," he says.

Alice decides she wants to climb into his lap, and he winces but he lets her.

"Alice, be careful," I say. "No kicking."

"I don't kick Samuel," she says solemnly.

My mother returns home with the yoke across her shoulders and two full buckets of water hanging from the ends. She is carrying a basket with four eggs in it. I help her unload the water buckets.

"I don't suppose we'll have to beg you to eat with us, Samuel," Mum says. She sounds a bit annoyed. It is the third day in a row, and Samuel's rations go to him now instead of to my father, the way they used to when Samuel still lived with us.

"Ginny, go to my cot in the barracks and reach under my mattress. You'll find a piece of salt pork wrapped in a rag," Samuel says. "I've been keeping it for a special occasion, and that must be today."

"Under your mattress?" Mum asks. "I'm surprised the dogs didn't find it." She breezes into the cottage to lay the table.

I leave them with Alice still bouncing on Samuel's knee, to retrieve the hidden treasure. When I return, my father has already come in from the fields for our midday meal. He picks Alice up and she giggles.

I go to check on Samuel's leg to see how the fresh air has been helping it to heal. I take one look and scream. The wound is filled with pale, wriggling maggots.

My mother comes running from inside the cottage. By now, Alice is crying, my father is laughing, Samuel is staring at his leg as if it might jump up and bite him, and I have one hand over my mouth to keep from vomiting. Mum takes Alice to calm her and examines Samuel's very lively wound.

"Oh, for heaven's sake, come and let's eat," Mum says, trying hard not to join my father in his laughter.

Samuel and I both look at her. "Eat?" I say in a weak voice.

"Yes, I'll pick them out later," she says. "In the meantime, let them do their work."

"Work?" Samuel asks. His face is ashen. He and I have both been reduced to one-word sentences.

"They will eat the dead tissue," Mum says. "It's the best thing to clean out infection."

I am too hungry to refuse dinner, and so is Samuel. While we eat, I make Samuel keep his leg under the table where I can't see it and I try not to think about those wriggly, squirmy maggots.

Ten

—

I HAVE A dream of ships.

It has the feel of the knowing, but it cannot be, dead as that is within me. Still, I wake shaking as if the ships were real.

They are frightful, fantastical, and strange. They come one after another, crowding the wharf at James Town. They unload their cargo: people. So many people. But not just ordinary groups of settlers. That is what is so odd. There are ships with only children, ships with all young women dressed in white dresses, and a ship carrying people with dark brown skin, dressed in colorful robes.

The people themselves are not frightful, but rather the sheer mass of them. They fill James Town to overflowing and spread up the river on both sides. Too many people to feed. Too many people to govern. Too many people spreading out into Indian lands, angering the Powhatan leaders.

I sit up in bed and shake my head to chase away the

dream. My nightclothes are wet, partly from my own sweat and partly because Alice has wet our bed again.

Alice opens her eyes.

"No more drinks of water at night for you," I tell her.

Gray dawn fills the cottage. My parents are two lumps in the bed next to ours.

I pull off my wet nightgown, and dress for the day in shift, petticoat, frock, and apron. Then I pull Alice's wet nightgown off her and dress her.

I use the bellows to fan the fire. The orange glow lights up the wooden table and chairs and the iron cook pot full of porridge. I use the ladle to break the crust that has formed on the porridge overnight and add some wood to the fire to get it going.

We are still only a few hundred settlers, I think, trying to wash away the dream. I hear my father yawn and use the chamber pot. He pulls on his clothes and boots. He'll need to get an early start. It's tobacco transplanting time. Though my father and Samuel are both skilled carpenters, ever since tobacco has become so important to the colony, they have been assigned to the tobacco fields during the planting, growing, and harvesting seasons. The carpenters work in the fields, and servants sleep in tents or out in the open for lack of good cottages.

"What have you got for me for breakfast today?" he asks as he sits at the table and runs his hands through his hair. "Roast pheasant?"

I laugh and ladle warm porridge into his bowl. "Roast pheasant is tomorrow," I say. "Today is porridge."

"Good. I like porridge, too," he says.

Mum was the first unmarried woman to ever come to James Town, and I can see why she chose my father over all the other men who tried to court her. He is tall, with lively eyes and a quick smile, and most important, he is kind through and through.

My father eats quickly and leaves for the fields. As my mother begins to stir, I have Alice help me carry our corn-husk mattress outside. We hang it on the laundry line, along with our nightclothes and linens, to dry.

"You're Mum's big girl now," I tell her. "When our new little sister comes, Mum will have enough diapers to wash and dry without our bed being wet every other night."

"I'll be her big sister?" Alice asks.

"That's right," I say.

My mother peeks her head out the cottage door. She is tying her apron over her big belly. "I heard that," she says. She is looking at me crossly.

I take Alice's hand and lead her back inside. "Heard what?" I ask innocently. I don't understand why she is angry with me.

"It's a girl?" she asks bluntly.

I feel the color rise to my cheeks. I look down. "I'm sorry, Mum," I say. Sorry that it's a girl, and sorry that I know.

Mum frowns. "Your father will get over it, and we'll try again," she says. "But *you*, you worry me, Virginia." She is mixing flour, water, salt, and yeast for our bread. I sit Alice at the table with her morning porridge.

"I'm trying, Mum," I say. "Sometimes it's just . . . *there*."

"That's what she said, too," my mother says softly.

A chill runs down my back. "My grandmother?" I ask. She nods.

Alice pretends to feed porridge to her rag doll.

"It is a gift and a curse," my mother says. "A gift from God, because I know your grandmother's heart was pure, and I know yours is, too, so where else could it come from?" She dumps the bread dough out onto a floured board and begins to knead it. "But it is a curse to have this gift and live among men who fear it." She stops her work and looks up at me. "Pray, Virginia. I know I told you to kill it in yourself, but that has not worked. You must ask God to take back this gift He has given you. Ask Him to take it from you so that your life may be spared."

"I will, Mum," I say earnestly. "I will pray."

* * *

I am on my way to fetch water, the yoke hanging from my shoulders. He steps into my path, blocking my way.

"No more rocks," he says.

I search Charles's face. There is not a hint of niceness

in it, only spite and determination. Could he really be calling a truce?

"When I was a boy, I threw rocks at you. I didn't know any other way. Now I am almost a man," he continues. He is not asking for a response from me. I try to move around him, but he easily blocks me and my yoke.

"Now all I have to do is watch you, until the time is right," he says. He narrows his eyes. "I know what you are. I know what your mother is." He straightens himself up. "The governor will listen to me when I make a report of witches among us."

I feel faint. I stumble forward but catch myself.

"You see?" Charles says, smiling with satisfaction. "Your guilt is all over your face."

I somehow gather myself enough to speak. "I am guilty of nothing," I say. "And neither is my mother. She tried to help your family, and your father, rest his soul, caused us nothing but grief." I shake my head. "Governor Yeardley will not listen to lies from a *boy*." I spit out the word "boy" and I see I have angered him. He picks up a stone and cocks his arm back, ready to throw it.

I turn my yoke sideways and push past him. As I walk away, I do not expect to feel the sting of a rock on the back of my head. Charles is too proud to help me prove my point.

• ✦ •

"Ship ashore!"

We are in the garden when we hear the shouts coming from the wharf. Alice's eyes brighten. "I want to go see!" she says. Even the smallest colonists know the excitement of landing ships.

I look to Mum for permission to leave our work.

"You girls go on," she says. "I'll finish up here."

Alice and I make a game of it, "racing" each other to see who can get to the wharf first. Of course, I take baby steps and let her win.

Others come to greet the ship as well, especially the gentlemen, who have servants to do their work for them and have nothing much to do except smoke their pipes, talk to one another, and occasionally go hunting. I hold Alice's hand and we listen to the conversations of the men around us as the ship sails closer.

"I hope they've sent the hogs Governor Yeardley requested. We'll need more than what we've got to stay well fed."

"I promised my wife I'd get her a coconut if they've any left over from their stop in the islands."

"Forget the coconuts, forget the hogs, I want a wife! I hope they've sent some unmarried women."

Lately, ships have been arriving in two and threes, but today there is only one ship for all these hopes to be pinned upon. She comes gliding in, her sails filled with the warm breeze. As she approaches the wharf, the sailors luff her sails. They toss lines to the men waiting onshore, and the ship is reeled in to dock. Her bow is painted in bright patterns of red, white, yellow, and blue. Her flags wave, stretched out flat and proud. *British*, the flags say with their white, red, and blue, *I am a British ship.*

It is odd, but there are no passengers on deck taking their first look at the shores of their new home. I think maybe the sailors are fed up with them always trying to come on deck, and they're making them stay down below in the 'tween deck until the last moment. I've heard many stories from Samuel about how hard it is to get a breath of fresh air on the journey to the New World.

Once the ship is close enough, the sailors lower the ramp. They begin rolling barrels and shoving crates down the ramp and onto shore. I have often complained, along with everyone else, that a new ship brings new mouths to feed—the mouths of people who know nothing about how hard they will have to work to survive here. But the thought of a ship without passengers is eerily strange. Where are all the people?

Alice has lost interest and is running toward two mastiffs who are sitting at the feet of their gentleman master. I don't know these dogs—they are new, and they are twice Alice's size—so I run after her. I scoop her up before she can reach them. She squawks her frustration. "I want to pet the dogs!" she cries.

Just then I hear a gasp and a murmur of voices. Someone says, "Oh dear, what has the Company done now?"

I turn to see what everyone else has already seen: there are, indeed, passengers, and they are finally being allowed to leave the ship. They come slowly down the wooden gangplank. Some are holding each other's hands. Some have faces set in scowls. Many are crying. Others simply have wide, fearful eyes. Their smell wafts to me on the breeze, of unwashed bodies and vomit. Their clothes are no more than rags.

They are children. Some are as small as six or seven years old, but there are no mothers or fathers with them. There are at least a hundred of them. And not a single one looks as though they have made this trip of their own free will.

Eleven

———

THESE CHILDREN ARE rough and wily and prone to fist fighting. They've been gathered off the streets of London and sent as free labor. They are orphans, runaways, children whose parents are too poor to feed them and who thought they could eat better living on the streets.

They begin to die almost immediately. They are sent to sleep in moldy tents or out in the open, some without even a blanket. Many are sent to the plantations upriver. All of them are put to work, from morning till night. And there is no one to take care of them, to make sure they get their rations.

One of the boys is different from the rest. He is nine or ten, and so quiet I realize after a couple of weeks that I have never heard him speak. When they first landed, I heard the pleadings of an older girl: "He wasn't even living on the street like the rest of us. He lived near the docks with his mum and da. His mum sent him to buy a sack of flour, and they grabbed him and shoved him onto the boat. He needs to be sent back home to his mum and da." But no one listened, and the ship set sail back to England without the boy.

He is sent to work in the tobacco fields each morning, and I see him return in the evening, his face dirty and sullen. I sneak, following him outside the fort one evening at dusk, and see him curl up with a torn old blanket, alone, staring at nothing and rocking his body to and fro. There is no food that I can see in his makeshift camp. Is he even bothering to get his rations?

This is what life has given you, I want to tell him. *You still have sunny days and the taste of food when you're hungry, and if you'd talk, you'd even have a few friends. You can't go back to England, but you can choose to be happy here.*

But I say nothing, and creep away silently, back to my own cottage, with my noisy family and lit candles and freshly baked bread with boiled turnips for supper.

Two weeks later, in the early morning, the boy is found cold and stiff in his blanket. Bermuda is sent to help dig the grave. When he returns to the fort, I meet him at the gates.

"We should have been his friends," I blurt out. I am surprised to hear anger in my own voice, as if I am blaming this on Bermuda.

"No, we couldn't," he says. "He wouldn't talk."

I kick at the dirt. "I wish I had at least tried to talk to him," I say.

"I . . . need to go put this shovel away," Bermuda says, and he hurries off before I can make him feel any more guilty.

Of all the hundred-odd children who came on that ship, the lucky ones are the older girls. The common men begin to court every girl over the age of thirteen, and soon we have weddings every Sunday. There is grumbling among the gentlemen and nobles. Why can't the Company send women from the upper classes for *them* to marry?

When Samuel doesn't find a girl to interest him among this new batch, I tease him. "Are you going to wait to see if the Company sends a duchess for you to marry?" I ask.

He laughs. "I'll know when it's the right one," he says. "There are more ships than ever these days. Lots to choose from."

I roll my eyes. "If you'll ever choose," I say.

A good thing about these new settlers is that one of the boys knows how to play the fiddle. We had a fiddle player in James Town, but he was shot in a hunting accident and died months ago. The new boy picks up the dead man's fiddle and immediately makes it come to life, playing songs that my parents say they used to hear at the street markets in England.

There is often someone on one of the ships who has brought along an instrument: a lute, a recorder, a flute, or a small drum. The noblemen play their gentle, lilting tunes on the lute. But the commoners, with their old, beat-up fiddles, flutes, and drums, many of them won in gambling games, come together to make rollicking music. The natives who live among us join in with their drums and rattles, and the music makes my feet want to dance. Now, with a fiddle to lead the melody, the musicians join each other more often to play in the evenings after work is done. I love going to sleep to the sound of lively songs being played and sung joyously by a make-shift band.

* * *

"Shhh." Samuel motions for me to follow him. He leads me to Governor Yeardley's house and pulls me to sit with him under the window. There is a heated discussion going on inside.

"Tobacco! That is all they sow, all they reap, all they want to grow—tobacco. Then comes the winter and they must trade with the natives for corn because they have not planted enough. They are hungry and sick all winter—and many die—for the sake of selling tobacco to England, and yet the money they earn cannot buy them meat here, it cannot buy them *life*. They are mad!" It is Governor Yeardley's voice.

"It is a difficult life here, sir. Many of them want nothing more than to earn their fortune in tobacco and return to England to escape this place."

"What of the ancients? Why have they not returned to England?" the governor asks.

"There are some who make their home here, sir. Indeed, some who would have nothing but servitude to return to."

"Life here does not have to be so difficult," says Governor Yeardley. "The orders have come from the Virginia Company of London to assign land to each family, one hundred acres to each of the ancients, half that for all the others. It is time for them to choose their land and prepare it. They will grow their own corn and pasture their cattle. If they are growing for their own table, then surely they will sow more than tobacco."

"Surely, sir."

"And the orders have come for them to have all the rights of Englishmen. Each settlement shall vote and elect representatives to speak for them. This way, each man shall have a voice in his own governance."

After that day, it is all I hear about. At the well fetching water, at the river washing clothes, walking through the fort, it is all anyone is talking about: We will have our own land. We will rule ourselves. Men who actually live in James Town and the outlying plantations and boroughs, and know the people's needs, will help to govern us. True, there will still be Governor Yeardley, appointed by the king, and a six-member council, appointed by the Virginia Company of London. But for the first time in

Virginia, there will be elections. Men, ages seventeen or older, who own land will vote to elect two representatives, or burgesses, from each borough and plantation. It will be a government of the people.

◆ ◆ ◆

I awaken to the sound of laughter in the street near our cottage. Laughter, loud talking in another language, and the rumble of bowling balls rolling along the dirt street.

I rub my eyes. My father is already up. "It's too early," I say, referring to the fact that bowling in the streets is only allowed after our work is done for the day.

"It's the Polish workers," my father says. "They're making it known that they will not work if they don't get to vote."

My mother is sitting on the side of their bed about to heft herself to her feet. This new baby will certainly arrive soon, as big as she is. "The Company won't be happy when there is no pitch or tar on the next ship back to England," she says. "I don't see what's wrong with letting those men vote. They are not Englishmen, but they are Virginians."

Alice kicks off the covers and I tickle her feet. "Da votes," she says, nodding solemnly.

We all laugh. She, too, has been paying attention to this talk of voting and burgesses, and of the land that my father and mother now own because they are ancients.

My father ruffles her hair. "Watch your mother today, girls," he says. "That son of mine may just choose this day to enter the world."

I smile at him. Maybe I was wrong. Maybe the knowing doesn't work for me anymore, now that God has taken it from me. Maybe my father will soon have a son.

I open the shutters to let in the early morning light. Then I fill a bowl with porridge for myself and Alice and we eat together.

My mother ties her apron over her large belly. "You two, go get me potatoes and cabbage. And see what is ready in the garden, too."

Outside I pull the wooden planks and the thick layer of straw off our storage hole. Inside are cabbages with their roots caked with dirt, still relatively fresh for having hidden underground all winter. The potatoes don't look as good—soft and wrinkled, with long white sprouts. I put Alice to work breaking off the potato sprouts and go to see what the garden might give us on this spring day. I cut some turnip greens and pull a handful of radishes. Alice and I carry it all inside for our mother.

A lump of salt pork—the last of our ration for the month—already sizzles in the stew pot. I love stew days. There will be enough for a full belly today.

I give Alice a bowl of water so she can wash the radishes, then my mother and I set to work peeling potatoes.

Every once in a while, she stops working and closes her eyes, just resting for a minute or so.

"Go get me fresh wild raspberry leaves," Mum says. "Fill the basket with them and when you come back, we'll make tea."

I remember the raspberry-leaf tea from the day Alice was born, only last time Jane made it.

"Shall I fetch Jane Wright as well?" I ask.

Mum shakes her head. "No, not yet."

I take the basket and run through the fort to the huge open gate.

"Where are you going in such a hurry?" Thomas Sexton, today's guard, calls to me.

"Going for raspberry leaves," I say.

I run past the fields where laborers are hoeing weeds from around the young tobacco plants. At the edge of the woods I see the raspberry brambles, but I am drawn first to enter the quiet of the forest. I pick my way over fallen logs and tiptoe around the ferns growing close to the ground. Then I stop to let the peacefulness sink into me. The wind rustles a few leaves. A birdcall echoes from the treetops. This is how I know I am more Virginian than English. English children have the treeless moors or the clamor of the streets of London. But I belong in the magic of the Virginia woods.

Suddenly I hear a twig snap. I whip around to catch

a glimpse of something white off behind thick oaks. It moves slowly, showing slivers of itself between trees and vines. It looks like . . . feathers. Could there really be a bird this big? I duck down low and creep along, following it, trying to get closer without startling it. This creature is neither bear nor wolf nor snake, and these are the only things in the forest that could kill me. Still, my heart races. I feel every muscle ready to flee as my curiosity moves me along, following.

Feathers. Wings—huge wings. Am I seeing something from the faery realm? Or an angel?

I draw closer and can see that the thing is walking on two legs. It moves silently, gliding. For a moment, I pay more attention to watching than to where I put my feet. I trip, crashing onto dry leaves. The thing stops and turns. I expect to see the beady eyes and yellow beak of this great bird. But instead what I see shocks me to my core: its face is human.

Twelve

I RUN, STUMBLING over roots and branches, my dress catching in brambles. I forget all about the raspberry leaves and run out of the forest, past the tobacco fields, into the gates of the fort, and burst into my own cottage. My mother stands at the fire, stirring the stew pot. She looks up in alarm.

"Mum, I just saw one of the faery folk—a huge one. Or an angel, I don't know which." I pant, out of breath.

Alice claps her hands. "Faeries?" she asks. I have told her stories of *good* faeries, not like the one I saw.

My mother sits me down and pours me a cup of water. "Tell me exactly what you saw," she says.

I describe the large white wings, the feathers on the thing's body, and the dark human face. My mother shakes her head. "An angel would not have scared you so. It must have been of the faery folk. There are those who come from the faery realm to steal human babies. This one may have come for this child." She touches her belly.

I shiver. "No, Mum. We can't let it."

She goes to my father's toolbox and pulls out iron tongs. She hands the tongs to me. "Take this with you in your basket. Those that are faery cannot abide iron. It will protect you. Once you have gathered the raspberry leaves, go to the sand pit where the men play that game with old horseshoes. Bring one of them back. They are made of iron as well."

A moment later she grips the edge of the table and closes her eyes. Beads of sweat form on her upper lip.

"I'll go get Jane Wright," I offer.

Mum takes a deep breath and relaxes. "Not yet," she says. "Jane has her own work to do." Then she frowns. "I thought the faery folk lived only in England. There you hear stories of an infant disappearing and nothing but a block of wood left in the cradle, or of changelings, where the human child is stolen and a faery creature is left in its place. I didn't know there were faery folk here in the New World. It is good that you were warned. We will be ready."

I put the iron tongs into my basket, alongside the knife for cutting the raspberry canes. This time I walk slowly, past the gates, past the fields, to the edge of the forest, where I find the wild raspberry brambles. I look into the cool darkness of the woods. The bird man is nowhere to be seen. *He doesn't want to steal me, he wants my baby sister*, I tell myself. I cut the raspberry canes, trying not to prick my fingers with their thorns. I fill my basket and run back to the fort before the bird man can reappear.

• • •

The raspberry tea sits brewing. Mum lays out clean rags and has me fill a pot with water to boil. When she has to stop her work to simply breathe, I rub the small of her back to help her feel better. Alice, knowing that something is different, keeps out of the way. She talks softly to her rag doll, saying, "Mum doesn't feel good today, so we have to be very quiet."

Finally, when my mother has to take to her bed, she says, "Go find Jane. Bring Alice with you—I would love to have you stay to help me, but I don't want Alice to be scared, so keep her away. But *don't* take her outside the fort."

Not with that creature out there, I think. I grasp Alice's hand and together we hurry to Jane Wright's cottage, where Jane is busy sewing.

"Mum sent me to fetch you," I say. "It's her time."

Jane puts down her sewing immediately. "Knowing your mother, she has waited until the last minute to call me and I'll have to run to get there on time," she says cheerfully. She picks up her bag and heads out the door.

With almost everyone in the tobacco fields, the fort

is quiet. I pick up a pretty white stone. "Alice, let's play a game." We sit down together on some logs near the big cook pot. "You have to guess where the stone is, all right?"

Alice nods as I put my hands behind my back. Then I pull my hands out, closed, and hold them in front of her.

"Handy dandy, prickly pandy, which hand will you have?" I chant. Alice chooses my right hand and I open it. She giggles when she finds the white stone inside. She tries to take it from me but I shake my head. "Let's play again," I say.

I hide my hands again, this time switching the stone to my left hand. "Handy dandy, prickly pandy, which hand will you have?"

Alice chooses my right hand again. When the hand is empty, she pouts and looks like she might be about to cry.

"Alice, it's a *game*," I tell her. "You'll get the prize sometimes, and get the empty hand sometimes, but it's supposed to be fun every time." I chuck her under the chin.

She looks at me gravely. "Fun every time," she says.

We play the game over and over, and Alice manages not to pout when she guesses wrong, though she only laughs when she is right. Finally, she begins to tire. "Let's go home now," she says.

"Not yet," I tell her. "We have to give Mum more time to rest."

The sun is sinking low and we hear the voices of the workers coming back from the fields.

Samuel comes into the fort, laughing and joking with his friends. But when he sees us, he comes over and whisks Alice into his arms. He is sweaty and dirty, but Alice doesn't mind. She makes her little hands into fists and says to him, "Pandy pandy, which hand?"

Samuel contemplates a moment, then points to her left hand. She opens her empty hand and giggles with glee.

"That's cheating, Alice," I say. "Both of your hands are empty."

"Sounds like some politicians I know," says Samuel.

My father comes in through the gates, looking as sweaty and dirty as Samuel. "Where is your mother?" he asks. "Is my son on his way?"

"Yes, Da, and she is well," I assure him. "Jane Wright is with her now."

"Good, good," my father says, though his eyes still look worried. I don't tell him about the faery creature who has come to try to steal this new baby. I know he has dark, sad memories of the baby who died after my mother was whipped, and I want him to have only hope for this new child.

Thirteen

————

THEY NAME HER Katherine. She is red-faced and scrawny, but my mother assures me she will be just as pretty as Alice and I are when she gets bigger. "Ah, three lovely daughters, and plenty of time for a son," my father says when he sees her.

That night I settle into bed with an iron horseshoe tucked under Alice's pillow. Katherine is in bed with our parents, the iron tongs forming a V above her head. There will be no babies stolen from this house tonight.

I lie awake thinking about the children who *were* stolen, rounded up from London and sent here against their will. There is talk of them becoming indentured servants, of them receiving their freedom and land when their seven years of service are over—those that survive, anyway. But I have seen how it goes with indentured servants. They somehow always end up in debt to their masters, and so freedom and land never come. My own mum was lucky that her mistress and master gave her permission to marry, and then when her mistress died, Mum was free to be a wife and mother without having to serve anyone.

I remember playing handy-dandy with Alice, and I think how those children got the empty hand. And I, with my mother and father and warm cottage, food to eat, and healthy sisters, have got the prize. As I drift off to sleep, I hear my own voice saying, *You'll get the prize sometimes, and get the empty hand sometimes, but it's supposed to be fun every time.*

• • •

Elections are held. Two men from each of the seven plantations and the four towns, including James Town, are elected as burgesses to represent the colonists. There are twenty-two burgesses in all.

Among the voters are the Polish craftsmen, and they are back at work making pitch, tar, and potash to be sent to England. The governor agreed to give them the right to vote, but on one condition: they must take on English apprentices and teach their craft to new young men. As soon as Bermuda hears this, he starts making a pest of himself with the Polish craftsmen. He insists that since the Polish workers were first sent here to make glass, "when" the glass house starts up again, they will be the ones making the glass. His plan is to be in the middle of all that and go right from making pitch and tar to blowing glass. I tell him he is dreaming, but he doesn't listen. The Polish men tell him he is too young to be an apprentice, that he'll burn his arm off in the tar pits, but he doesn't listen to them, either.

If the Poles appreciate persistence, Bermuda will soon have his place as an apprentice. If they do not appreciate persistence, Bermuda will soon be banished from their sight. In the meantime, his mother constantly complains that he's never around to do his chores. And I complain that he never goes fishing with me anymore.

The days grow long and hot. Mosquitoes buzz around my head whenever I weed the garden or sit grinding corn. More and more people fall ill with the summer flux, and Bermuda is dragged away from the tar pits to help dig graves. In the midst of it all, baby Katherine grows fat on my mother's milk, and even starts to look a little bit pretty.

On Friday, July 30, the General Assembly has its first official meeting in the church in James Town. In attendance are the twenty-two elected burgesses, the governor and his six-member council, Reverend Buck, and the colony's secretary, John Pory. When Samuel leaves for the tobacco fields in the morning, he tells me to go listen to the meeting from outside the church windows. He says it is an important day, and I should witness it.

Reverend Buck opens with a prayer, and the meeting begins. The most interesting part is when a case is brought against John Martin, who is accused of stealing corn from the Indians. Governor Yeardley stresses how important it is for all colonists to treat the Indians with respect and kindness, in order to keep the peace we now have. He says that absolutely no robberies will be tolerated. I am very happy to hear the governor say this. If everyone keeps the peace, then surely the dreaded third battle from the prophecy will never come to pass.

The General Assembly was to meet all week, but one after another, the men fall ill with the summer flux. One of the burgesses dies. And so the meeting is cut short, but not before the assembly makes many important decisions. They lay out the specifics about how the hundred-acre plots will be assigned to the ancients. They enact laws against drunkenness, idleness, and gambling. I also hear them talking about the colony's first tax, which is to be paid to *them*.

When I tell Da about the tax, Alice wants to know what a "tass" is.

"Those men are making laws for us," Da says, "and so we all pay them for doing that."

"Why are they making the poor servants pay the same as the rich land owners?" I ask him.

Da doesn't look up from the chair he is repairing. "I suppose we're paying them to make laws, not to be fair," he says.

The General Assembly adjourns on August 4. The tax

is collected: one pound of the best tobacco from every man and every servant in the colony, paid to the assembly members for, as one hot, sweaty field-worker says, "having sat in the cool of the church and talked for five days."

• • •

On Sunday afternoon after church services, my mother sends me to go fishing. Bermuda is catching up on a week's worth of chores for his mother, and so I am going alone. With my worms in a bucket and my fishing stick over my shoulder, I walk through the fort toward the gates.

Sunday is the day for visiting and trading, and there are many natives in the fort with their baskets of bread, meat, and dried berries for trade. Samuel stands in a circle with Choupouke, a young Indian man who lives in James Town, and two visiting native men. The four of them are speaking Algonquian. When Samuel sees me, he calls me over.

"Bring us back some trout. Can't you see we're starving at the soldiers' barracks?" he says.

The other men laugh—they obviously understand enough English to get Samuel's humor.

I shake my head. "Mum will want me to bring her anything I catch. Are you too lazy to do your own fishing?"

Samuel pretends to nearly faint. *"Mowchick woyawgh tawgh noeragh kaquere mecher?"* (I am very hungry; what shall I eat?)

Now he is clowning for his friends, and I don't like not knowing what he is saying. I decide to show off one of the Algonquian words I do know. "I'm not giving you any of my *noughmass*. Go catch your own *noughmass*."

Samuel laughs, grabs me, and tickles me.

"Samuel, let me go." I struggle to free myself from his grasp, but he holds on tight.

"*Netoppew?*" he asks.

"Yes, we're still friends," I say. "Just let me go fishing before my mother decides I've got other chores to do."

The next moment I look up and gasp. The creature's white wings shine bright in the sun, the feathers on his body lift in the breeze, and his dark face is set with determination. The bird man has just walked through the gates into the fort.

Fourteen

—

"LET ME GO! I have to warn Mum!" I cry, but Samuel still holds me tight. I sink my teeth into his arm.

Samuel sets me loose with a shove that sends me sprawling onto the ground. "Have you gone mad?" he says, rubbing his arm. "I was just playing."

The bird man is now walking quickly toward me. I panic, scramble to my feet, try to run, but Samuel grabs me. "Stop being rude!" he says, and jerks my arm.

The creature has not only a human face, but the arms and legs of a human as well. I hear Algonquian words spoken behind me. "*Wingapo, Nemattanew.*"

The creature nods. "*Wingapo,*" it says.

Wingapo. It is the word of greeting among *netoppew*, among friends.

Samuel speaks to the bird man in Algonquian, then he looks at me sternly and says, "I told him no wonder the English bullets cannot hurt him—they are afraid of him like little girls. Now you must show respect. Nemattanew is a great, honored warrior."

I look from Samuel to the bird man and back again. An honored warrior? A *man*, not a creature of the faery realm? I let out a shaky breath. "*Wingapo*," I say. Nemattanew nods to me. Then he speaks to Samuel in Algonquian.

"Ah," Samuel says. "He tells me you saw him in the *musses*, the woods, a while back, that you were alone and were afraid of him and ran away."

I feel my face turn red with embarrassment. How could I have been so silly to think he was a faery creature come to steal my sisters?

"Well, you only need to be afraid of him if you want to fight him in a battle," Samuel says. Then he rattles off something in Algonquian that makes the whole circle of men laugh.

I blush again. "Can I go now?" I ask. I am trying to be polite, but I want very much to be done with this.

"Nobody is stopping you," Samuel says.

As I hurry away, I hear my name called out in a gruff voice with a heavy Algonquian accent. I stop and turn. Nemattanew is looking at me.

He lifts his chin toward me, then he takes one finger and touches it to the center of his forehead. The gesture sends a chill down my back.

To make things worse, Charles has been watching this whole interaction. As I leave the fort, my worm bucket swinging and my fishing stick in hand, he follows me.

"I saw you with that Indian warlock," he calls after me.

I keep marching down the hill toward the river, trying to ignore him.

"I heard him say your name," Charles says, catching up to me. "Do you do your evil rituals with him in the forest?"

I wheel around to face him. I don't even know how to begin to respond to these insane accusations.

"Ah, so you *do* have rituals with him in the forest." Charles raises his eyebrows.

I want badly to punch him but I stop myself. "I just met him today," I say as calmly as I can. "And he is a great *warrior*, not a *warlock*. You should check to see if there are balls of wax in your ears."

At the river's edge, I pull a worm out of my bucket and stab it onto my fishhook. Charles watches me.

"Don't you ever do any work?" I demand.

He raises his head high. "I am a gentleman," he says.

If Captain Smith were still here, Charles would be working. When he was president, Captain Smith didn't let the gentlemen be idle the way they are in England, and the way they are becoming here.

Charles gets bored with watching me fish and decides

to leave me alone. Halfway up the hill, he calls back to me, "You just wait. I'll have plenty to report to the governor."

My stomach clenches. But then I comfort myself with the thought that Governor Yeardley will not likely put me on trial just because an Indian warrior spoke my name.

• • •

My mother has been assigned to make coats for the laborers of the colony. This time, Governor Yeardley has made sure she has good cloth and good thread, and even new needles. She is proud of her work. While Katherine sleeps, Alice and I sit with Mum. Alice practices her sewing on a scrap of cloth, and I sew the hems on the coats, making my stitches as straight and neat as I can.

Alice looks up from her crooked stitches. "Da is coming home," she says.

"Yes, sweetheart," Mum says. "He'll be home later at noon for dinner."

Alice shakes her head. "No, he's coming home now."

Mum and I exchange a look. I tense inside. A few minutes later, we hear Da's whistle as he walks through the fort toward our cottage. Mum goes pale.

I lean in to Mum's ear and whisper quickly, "Don't worry. When she gets a little older, we'll tell her to ask God to take it away from her, the way I have, and it will be gone forever, the way it is for me."

Da bursts in through the door. "I've got the map!" he declares. "The map of our land."

He plops a piece of paper down on the table, in the midst of our sewing. It is a crudely drawn map that looks like winding snakes. I realize the snakes must be the rivers, flowing through the land.

"Here is James Town," Da says, pointing. "And see this? This is Point Comfort, and here's Kecoughtan, or Elizabeth City as they're now calling it." He runs his finger over places that are down the James River from James Town. "And this"—he points, then looks up at us—"this is *our* land. One hundred acres." It has been inked in, a long rectangle, not near James Town, but down the river near Elizabeth City.

My mother touches the place on the map he has pointed to. She looks up at my father in amazement. "I was a servant girl," she says. "Now I am a landowner." She shakes her head slightly. "It is the *New* World."

Da's eyes are bright. "I want to start clearing and building a house as soon as the tobacco harvest is over," he says.

That's when it actually hits me. "We're moving?" I ask.

"Of course," my father says. "We're moving to our own land."

Leaving James Town? Leaving our cottage? "But . . ." I must be able to come up with an objection that will stop this nonsense. "We'll be outside the fort gates. It will be dangerous."

My father pats my arm. "Don't worry, Virginia, we are at peace with the natives, so we don't need the fort walls anymore. There are plenty of settlements up and down the river now, and they are safe."

I hear Samuel's voice from years ago, *How long do you think the peace will last with her gone?*

I am still scowling. How can he ask me to leave the only home I've ever known?

My father continues with his news. "Samuel will be coming with us. We've decided to join our acreage and share the two hundred acres that gives us."

What about Bermuda? What about our home, our cottage? What if the Spanish attack, and there we are, right at the mouth of the river? What if the peace with the Indians doesn't last?

Alice is climbing up onto the table to better see the map. "This is our land, Da?" she asks. "This right here?" She goes to pick up the paper, but Mum rescues it from her grasp. Da pulls Alice onto his lap. "This is a *picture* of our land. Our real land is out there." He sweeps his arm to the south. "It has trees we can cut to build a house with, good soil for a garden and tobacco, turkeys and deer we can kill for meat, and grass for when we get a cow. It has everything we need." Alice nods, her face full of wonder.

I sigh. At least Alice is excited about our move.

After supper, I am still grumpy. I put a dry diaper on Katherine and swaddle her. I help Alice change into her nightgown. All the while I am feeling dark and sad about this move.

My mother puts her arm around me. "Get some sleep, Virginia," she says gently. "It will all look better in the morning."

• • •

Samuel comes over early the next day before he has to leave for the fields.

"Da says we're joining our land together," I say, trying not to sound too sullen.

He nods. "And do you like our choice of location?" he asks.

I cock my head to the side. "Land is land, isn't it?"

"Don't you remember?" he asks. "This land is like a good-luck charm. Point Comfort was where your family and I were well fed while almost everyone in James Town starved to death."

"When I was a baby," I add. It is a story I've heard many times, but I didn't realize they had chosen our land to be close to the place that saved us that winter.

"We're hoping it will bring us good luck again," Samuel says.

I narrow my eyes at him. "In case everyone starves to death again?" I am only joking, so I'm surprised when Samuel takes my comment seriously.

"Sure," he says. "There were lots of horseshoe crabs there to eat last time."

"Good morning, Master Collier," Da says.

Samuel laughs. "I wouldn't go that far," he says. "The New World can't make me into a gentleman. But it turns out Reverend Hunt was right."

"Right about what?" I ask.

Samuel gets a faraway look. "Just before he died," he says, "Reverend Hunt told me I would not always be a servant. He said I would be something much greater than that. I never dreamed I'd be a landowner."

"And don't forget, you're also our best interpreter," Mum says.

"Don't forget, you're also a smelly field-worker," I say.

He tries to punch me in the arm, but I jump out of the way. Samuel leaves to work in the fields, and I go out to our garden to harvest and weed before the day gets too hot.

It is late August, and the heat has settled in like an itchy wool blanket. In the afternoon, the little ones are napping and my mother is busy at her sewing. I ask if I may go down to the river to dunk my head in and cool off.

The air is filled with the chirping and whirring of

crickets and cicadas. It surprises me when I get to the river and see a lone ship sailing in. No one has given the shout of "Ship ashore!"

She approaches slowly, her sails only barely filled. There is a groggy haziness to the day. *Are the watchmen asleep?* I wonder.

A few gentlemen stand, watching, smoking their pipes. As the ship draws nearer, I expect to see the familiar Union flag: the red cross of St. George against the white cross of St. Andrew with the blue background. But when I see the flag it is flying, fear grips me. It is not a British flag.

We have all been warned to keep a watch for ships flying the Spanish naval jack because a Spanish ship would most likely mean attack. But this flag is neither British nor Spanish. It has three wide horizontal swaths of orange, white, and blue. I overhear the gentlemen's conversations.

"It is a Dutch ship."

"No, it's an English warship."

"Nonsense. She flies the Dutch colors."

"An English captain who wants the freedom to attack Spanish or Portuguese ships, and steal their cargo, without enraging our peace-making king, will fly the Dutch colors. It is an English ship."

I watch curiously as this ship, flying its impostor colors, comes nearer. Finally, someone calls out, "Ship ashore!" and a few watchmen stagger down to the wharf to help the ship dock. The captain calls out a greeting in perfect, unaccented English. The conversations onshore continue.

"Ah, the *White Lion*. That ship saw many a bloody battle with the Spanish during the war."

"Her captain must still be causing a ruckus at sea. I wonder what he has stolen?"

"Whatever it is, he will certainly want to sell it to us."

The gangplank is lowered. But there are no crates or barrels to unload. No cattle or hogs to lead to shore to sell.

As I watch, I feel as though I am back in the dream, the dream of ships. Because what I see cannot be real. Led down the gangplank, with chains around their necks and ankles, are people. About twenty of them. Men, women, and children with skin the color of brown butterflies, dressed in tattered robes of orange, yellow, and indigo.

The conversations onshore are hushed, but one word stands out: *slaves*.

People. For sale.

Fifteen

———

THEY ARE ENSLAVED Africans, stolen from a Portuguese slave ship. They had first stopped at Point Comfort and were sent along to James Town. Governor Yeardley buys them in exchange for the food the crew of the *White Lion* needs for their trip back to England. They now belong to the colony.

The Africans are taken out of their chains and sent to the hot tobacco fields to work alongside the London street children, indentured servants, and other commoners like Samuel and my father. Tobacco is queen, we commoners are her servants, and the gentlemen reap the profits.

Samuel says that James Town is becoming more and more like England. He says that when Captain John Smith was president, even the gentlemen had to work in the fields if they wanted to eat. But now the gentlemen have servants in their homes to do the women's work and servants in the fields to do the farmwork, and they sit puffing on their pipes while their wives gossip with the other gentlewomen.

"We won't be like that when we get our land," Samuel promises me. "We know the value of hard work."

"Yes, and we can't afford servants," I remind him.

A few days after the landing of the *White Lion*, another ship arrives at Point Comfort carrying more stolen slaves. This ship not only flies the British colors, but it is a ship well known to us: the *Treasurer*. Captain Argall used the *Treasurer* to capture Pocahontas and bring her to James Town, and he carried her to England aboard it. According to the Powhatans, it is the ship on which Captain Argall gave Pocahontas the deadly poison that took her life.

The *Treasurer* is now involved in more intrigue. Her captain, Daniel Elfrith, sailing under the British colors, did not have permission to plunder Spanish ships. His stolen slaves are contraband and he can be accused of piracy. The residents of Point Comfort want nothing to do with him, his slaves, or his request for food. He leaves without trading anything or anyone. But not before one of his "contrabands" jumps ship and runs off into the forest.

A few colonists catch a glimpse of her as she runs, and soon everyone is talking about her. Why is she not in chains like the others? What is she so desperate to escape by running off into an unknown forest? Is she a Christian, like the slaves from the *White Lion*, who have baptismal names like John, Mary, Peter, and Margaret? Will Captain Elfrith come back for his stolen "property" and risk arrest for piracy? Rumors spread quickly, reaching James Town that very same day. Some say she is very beautiful and was Captain Elfrith's mistress on board the ship. Some say she has scars and must have been mistreated on the ship. Some say it was so blasted hot, she must have thought they were back in Africa and she could run home. By the end of the day, everyone has an idea about who she is and what she is thinking. But no one knows where she has gone.

That night I lie awake in the heat. I think about the young woman lost in the forest. Is she afraid? Is she lonely? Has she found water to drink? Does she know which berries and roots are good to eat? How long can she live out there by herself? What will the Indians think of her if they find her? Will they welcome her into their tribe to live, the way they did with Samuel when he was a boy?

Each day search parties go into the forest to look for her. Each day they come back without her.

On Sunday during church, Reverend Buck exhorts the congregation to pray for the "young Christian woman" lost in the woods. "If she starves and dies," he says, "her blood will be on our hands."

I do exactly as he says. I sit in the cool of the church,

and as Reverend Buck continues his sermon, I pray for her, that God will keep her safe until we can find her. I pray that He will somehow let her know that we colonists will not harm her.

As I sit quietly, an image comes to me: a creek with boulders alongside it; a break in the boulders that is the entrance to a small cave. It feels a little bit like the knowing, but there is not enough information to tell me anything, and the knowing has been dead in me for a long time now, so I ignore the image and go back to praying.

Reverend Buck's sermon drones on. I get sleepy but work hard to keep myself awake—I don't want to anger Reverend Buck. My head droops and as I snap it up, the image comes again. This time it has the unmistakable *ping* of the knowing. My heart races. If I focus, will I be able to see where the creek is? Will I be able to find the lost African woman?

It is then that I do a very bad thing. *Lord, please help me find her*, I pray. I am asking God for more knowing rather than to keep the knowing from me.

Immediately, the image in my mind sharpens. I see that the creek runs into the river where a large oak has been hit by lightning and is cracked and charred down its middle. I suck in my breath. Samuel, in the pew next to me, nudges me and questions me with his eyes. I scowl at him. The punishment for talking during church is very painful.

I bow my head again. It is there, clear as the living day: the creek, the oak, the boulders, the cave. I can find the young woman, I am sure of it.

I am also sure, to my horror, that I have opened the door to the knowing again, and it is with me, stronger than ever. My heart pounds in my ears. I can save the young African woman's life. But my life is now in danger.

Sixteen

AFTER CHURCH SAMUEL drags me away from the crowd of worshippers.

"What?" he asks simply. He knows me well.

"I can find her," I whisper.

He glances around furtively, making sure no one can hear. "I'll go with you. Is it over land or water?"

"Water. We need a canoe," I say.

He thinks a moment. "Go tell your mother I'm taking you fishing. Then go home and find any food you can. I'll meet you where the fishing canoes are docked."

At our cottage, I wrap stale bread and summer apples in a cloth sack. It is now or never. Sunday is the only day we can get away from work, and in a week, the African woman may well be dead from hunger.

Samuel has brought along two fishing sticks to make the fishing trip official. As we push the canoe into the river, he asks, "Upstream or down?"

The moment he asks it, I know. "Downstream," I say.

We paddle out into the current and then let the river do most of the work. We watch the landscape glide by, Samuel paddling and steering in the back of the canoe, me in the front. We both search the shoreline for the lightning-damaged oak.

At first, I am excited, like a cat ready to spring, expecting to find the oak right away and race up the creek to find the woman. But as time passes, and we paddle in silence, the quiet rush of the river makes my mind wander. I wonder if this will be the end of me. Will Charles figure out that I used the knowing to find the African woman, and accuse me of being a witch? Will Governor Yeardley believe him? Or will Nemattanew come back to James Town, touching the middle of his forehead and telling everyone that the Indian god Ahone has given me the gift of the second sight? Will I be branded a devil worshipper? I imagine the pyre, lit to burn me, and the strangling cord. . . .

"Virginia, what is it?" Samuel's voice is urgent.

It shakes me out of my morbid thoughts. "What is what?"

"Why did you moan like that?"

I am shocked to realize I moaned out loud. I take a deep breath. If I can trust anyone with my thoughts, it's Samuel. "Do you think the Powhatans worship the devil, the way Reverend Buck says?" I ask.

Samuel dips his paddle into the water and pulls, dips

and pulls. "They marry and they love their children the way we do. They play games and create music and dances the way we do. They have laws the way we do and punish those who break the laws the way we do. When they fight their wars, they have rules about it, the way we do. They share their food with each other and are kind to their animals and respect their elders. I don't see how they can be so much like us and be devil worshippers. Maybe they worship the same God as we do, and just have a different name for Him. That's what I think," he says. Then he adds quickly, "But you can't tell anyone I said that."

"I won't tell," I promise.

"Why do you ask?"

"Because that day Nemattanew came to James Town, as I was leaving, he spoke to me with his hands. I am almost certain that he spoke of the knowing. Even though I thought it was gone, he saw that it was still there."

Samuel is silent, and I listen to the swish of our paddles in the river.

I continue. "If Nemattanew knows I have it, and if that means that it comes from their god and not ours, then I must be possessed by the devil, just like they said about my grandmother." There, I've said it.

Suddenly I feel a shower of cold water against my back. I swing around. Samuel splashes me with his paddle again, this time in the face.

"Hey, stop!" I splash my paddle into the river and send

a spray of water at him, but more water ends up in the boat than on him.

"Don't sink us!" he shouts, but he is laughing, and by now I am laughing, too.

"Virginia, you being possessed by the devil is the most ridiculous thing I have ever heard," he says. "I don't know if Okeus or Ahone or the Great Spirit have anything to do with our God, and I don't know what Nemattanew was really saying to you that day. But I will ask you this: Where were you today when you had your vision about how to find the young African woman?"

"In church," I say quietly.

"Exactly. The devil doesn't go to church. I think God is trying to tell you that it is a gift from Him, and that you are to use it to serve Him."

For a moment, Samuel's words make me feel light inside, as if a great burden has been lifted. But then I feel the darkness again. "That boy Charles . . ." I begin.

"That boy who has nothing better to do than torment younger children?" Samuel asks.

"Yes, that one. He is determined to prove that Mum and I are witches. He has that in his head because his da told him about my grandmother in England."

"He has no proof of anything," Samuel says.

"But what if he finds out how I knew where to find the African woman?" I ask.

"You mean what if he finds out that you and I were out fishing together and happened to come across her?"

Samuel is right. Charles has no proof of anything. When I turn to thank Samuel, I see it: the lightning-split oak. We are drifting past it.

"That's it—we're here!" I cry. "Paddle to shore!"

Seventeen

———

WE PADDLE THE canoe to shore and I jump out. I grab the cloth sack that holds our bread and apples.

"Wait," says Samuel. "Let me give you some Spanish words to say to her."

I huff. "Samuel, I don't have time for jokes." I hurry toward the creek bed.

"I'm not making a joke," he says. "Come back."

I march back to him and cross my arms over my chest. "So, you're saying that Africans speak Spanish, *and* you speak three languages, and I'm supposed to believe it's not a joke?" I am impatient. "Hurry up," I say. "She might be about to starve to death."

"The other Africans speak some Spanish because they're from the kingdom of Ndongo, where there are lots of Spanish and Portuguese," Samuel says. "I learned from them how to say 'Good day.' If you greet her in Spanish and she understands you, she'll feel at home."

"All right. I'm ready," I say. I've learned a little bit of Algonquian, so why not Spanish?

"When you find her, just say *buenos días*," he says. He sounds it out for me "*Bwe-nos dee-as.*"

"*Bwe-nos dee-as,*" I say. "Can I go now?"

"Go," he says. "I'll catch a few crayfish for bait and do some fishing."

I pick my way up the side of the creek, sometimes hopping onto rocks to avoid thick brush growing along the banks. I practice as I go, "*Bwe-nos dee-as.*" Now I know how to say a greeting in three languages: Good day. *Wingapo. Buenos días.*

As I make my way, I watch for any sign of the boulders I saw in my mind's eye. I begin to wonder about what I'll really find when I reach the cave. The decaying body of someone already dead? An injured person in need of a splint or herbs? A woman so crazed with hunger and fear that she runs from me? Or will I find no one? Will I never find the boulders and cave at all? Has this all been a game of my imagination?

I suddenly feel like a ridiculous young girl. Brambles catch on my leg and tear my skin. "Ow!" I say out loud, and wipe blood from the scratch. I sit down hard on a rock near a calm pool of the creek. I feel so foolish. I've brought Samuel all this way because of a daydream I had in church. And even if I do find the woman, what are the chances she'll even be willing, or able, to come back with us? I hang my head. Then I cup my hands into the creek and take a drink, causing ripples to go out in all directions. As I look into the water, the surface becomes calm again and I see my own reflection with trees and clouds above. "You've gone mad, Virginia," I say to the face in the water. "Go get Samuel, go fishing, and go home. Be done with this nonsense."

Suddenly another face appears in the reflection behind me. It is a dark, menacing face.

I scream. I hear another blood-chilling scream. I scramble to my feet, try to run, slip on the rocks, and fall into the water.

Then I hear something I do not expect: laughter.

She is slender and tall, hardly older than a teenager. She has arching eyebrows and bright eyes, and she is studying me.

I stand up, dripping wet. I stare at her. Her head is wrapped in a swath of beautiful patterned indigo cloth. Her body is wrapped in similar cloth, torn in several places, draped over one shoulder, with her arms bare. She seems to be neither sick nor injured and she definitely isn't running away. On her ankles and wrists are the same scars I've seen on the other slaves that were brought to James Town: scars from the chains she was kept in during the months-long passage from Africa on the Portuguese slave ship.

She makes the fierce grimace she made when I saw her in the reflection, then points to me and mimics my scream. Then she's off into another round of laughter. I am still shaken up, but I laugh a little, too. It is, after all, funny.

Suddenly I remember the words I'm supposed to say to her. "*Buenos días*," I say

Her eyes light up. "*Buenos días*," she answers.

I decide to try to introduce myself. I tap my chest. "Virginia," I say.

She nods, sets her fist against her own chest, and says, "Ndongo."

But Ndongo is the name of a kingdom, the place Samuel thinks she is probably from. Then I realize that Virginia is the name of a place as well. She must have heard, on the English ship, that they were going to Virginia, and she thinks I'm saying I'm *from* Virginia.

I begin to shake my head, to correct her, when I remember something much more important: the food I've brought for her, tied in a sack to my apron. I open the sack and pull out a soggy piece of bread. I hold it out to her. It drips a bit.

She reaches to receive the food. "Thank you," she says.

She must have learned some English during her time on the *Treasurer.* I hand her an apple as well and decide to try again with the introductions.

"My name is Virginia," I say, pointing to myself.

She points to herself. "My name, Angela."

A Christian name. She is a Christian, then, just as Reverend Buck said.

Angela eats sitting on a rock. As I watch, my own stomach growls, but I know that Angela has been without food for longer than I have.

The next thing is to convince her to come with us. "I have a boat," I begin. "I can take you—"

Angela's eyes flash. "No boat!" She puts up one hand, resisting.

I shake my head. "No, not the ship that brought you here. It is gone." I use hand motions to better clarify my words. "I have a little boat." I show *small*, a space of a yard between my hands. "A canoe with paddles." I make a paddling motion.

She looks more relaxed, but still wary.

"We can go back to James Town, get more food, and some rest." I motion paddling, eating, sleeping.

Angela frowns as she chews the apple. She seems to be considering my offer. Of course, I can't be sure she has understood. I motion for her to follow me, and I start down along the creek. We can't dally. Sunset is only a few hours away and we have a long way to paddle upstream.

I look back. She has not moved from the rock she is sitting on, but she is watching me. What more can I do? I still have an apple and another piece of soggy bread in my sack. The least I can do is help her not to starve. I go back and give her the food.

"I'm going to the boat—I mean the canoe. You can come if you want," I tell her. Then I begin the hike down to where Samuel is waiting for me. Angela does not follow.

When I reach Samuel, he is just pulling a smallmouth bass out of the river on his fishing line. "Did you find her?" he asks.

"Yes. But she wouldn't come with me. She knows some English, and when I told her we have a boat, I think she was afraid it was the ship that brought her here."

"Is she hurt or sick?" he asks.

"No, and she must have been finding things to eat, because she doesn't even seem weak. And of course, there is plenty of water from the creek. But she was hungry enough to eat the food I brought even though the bread was soaking wet."

Samuel raises his eyebrows. "What did you do, drop it in the creek?"

"It's a long story," I say. Then, to change the subject, "We need to head back; it's getting late."

But Samuel will not miss this opportunity to tease me. "Mmmm. Nothing like wet bread to whet your appetite, I always say."

"Samuel, can we just go?" I plead.

"Yes, of course, Miss Laydon," he says. "And would you like some of our delicious creek-soaked bread to eat while we travel?"

"All right, fine," I say, knowing he won't stop until I've told him everything. "She came up behind me and scared me and I fell into the creek. Now are you satisfied? Can you stop teasing me now?"

But he isn't looking at me. He is looking behind me. He stands up slowly and raises his arms—the motion the Indians make when they are showing us they have no weapons.

I freeze, afraid to look. I expect him to call out a greeting of friendship, to protect us from attack. I wait for him to say "*Wingapo*" or "*Netoppew*." But he doesn't.

Finally, he does call out a greeting.

"*Buenos días!*"

Eighteen

ANGELA STANDS, TALL and serious. Her eyes dart around. She is looking for anyone who might grab her and put her back in chains. It has taken tremendous courage for her to come find us.

Samuel crosses his arms over his heart. "Friends," he says. "Don't be afraid."

Angela comes a few steps closer. She points to the canoe. "Boat?" she asks.

"Yes, that's the boat I was telling you about," I say. "A canoe."

She shows an inch between her thumb and forefinger. "Boat," she says in a high voice. She is saying our boat is tiny. Hopefully, she is also saying she has no reason to fear it, or us.

"Will you come home with us?" I ask her, making the paddling motion. "Where we can eat, and rest?" I show her *eat* and *sleep*. It is getting late. If we don't start paddling very soon, we won't be back before dark. "Let's go," I say to Samuel.

Samuel and I go to the canoe. Samuel picks up a rock and gives the flopping bass a sharp knock to the head to kill it, then tosses it and our fishing sticks into the boat. We push it partway into the water and Samuel gets in. I motion to Angela. She hesitates a moment, then she seems to take an inner leap of faith and comes to join us. She balances expertly, and I wonder if they have canoes in her homeland.

I push us free of shore and hop in. We are taking Angela back to James Town.

We keep to the edge of the river where the current is weaker. I sit at the front, with Samuel at the rear and Angela in the middle between us. At first, we paddle in silence. Then Samuel asks, "Are you from Ndongo?" And the two of them are off on a conversation that uses English, along with words I don't understand that must be either Spanish or her language, and hand motions that I keep turning around to see until Samuel tells me I'm rocking the canoe too much. "You just paddle, and I'll tell you what her hands say," he tells me.

And so, Angela's story takes shape. She was captured during a war with the Portuguese—they were taking over Ndongo land. A very bad tribe of people, the Imbangala, fought alongside the Portuguese and captured the good people of Ndongo to sell them into slavery. She is from the nobleman class. She was stolen away from her husband and baby daughter. She will never see them again, and her heart is broken. But God wants her to live. That is why she is coming with us—so she will not starve.

I scowl. That wretched ship, the *Treasurer*, has once again taken a young mother away from her child.

"What will they do with her in James Town?" I ask Samuel when Angela's story has ended.

"Put her to work like anyone else, give her a place to sleep and food to eat like anyone else. There's not much difference among us common folk," he says.

"Do you think they'll send her off to the tobacco fields at one of the boroughs?" I ask. I hope they won't. I hope Angela will stay in James Town so that I can get to know her more.

Angela makes a clicking noise with her mouth.

"She's shaking her head," says Samuel. "She must have understood your question about working in the fields. Maybe since she is from a noble family, working in the fields would be beneath her. . . . Yes, she's making motions; sewing, cooking, these are the things she is willing to do."

"Do you think they'll let her choose?" I ask.

"I'll see what I can do," Samuel says.

The sun is sinking low. My arms ache terribly.

"Hey, keep up the pace," Samuel says. "We need to get back before dark or your mum will worry."

I groan.

"Virginia." It is Angela speaking to me.

I turn to look at her. She raises her eyebrows, opens her hands, motions to my paddle.

"Go ahead. Give it to her," Samuel says.

Angela moves closer to me and I gladly hand the paddle to her. She sets to work with strong, swift strokes.

"Yes. Now we'll make it home," says Samuel.

I am slightly annoyed by the insult, but in truth I don't know how much longer I could have kept going, and we are far from home. I scoot down low in the canoe, rest my head on my knees, and doze off.

．．．

There is quite a commotion when we arrive in James Town at dusk. Everyone says how lucky we were to find Angela near our fishing spot. Reverend Buck offers prayers of thanks that a Christian woman has been saved from starvation. Governor Yeardley paces, totally confused about what to do with this person who was supposed to be a slave, but for whom no money has been paid, and so she is not a slave. Men, commoners and gentlemen alike, stare. Just like the rumors said, Angela is quite beautiful, with long, graceful arms and dark, flashing eyes.

Samuel explains that she is nobility and cannot be sent to be a field-worker, and this confuses Governor Yeardley even more. I stand with Angela, feeling protective of her.

She seems to be understanding some of what is going on, but mostly she looks overwhelmed.

I notice Joan Pierce talking to her husband, Captain William Pierce, and motioning toward Angela. Finally, Captain Pierce marches over to Governor Yeardley and speaks to him.

"My wife says we will bring her into our home. She may work alongside our other servants and share a bed with Ester, our maidservant," he says.

I look at Angela to see if she has understood. "Will you go with them?" I ask quietly. "They live here in James Town, in a nice cottage. They are good people." I want to add, *Then I'll get to see you every day*, but I don't.

Captain and Mrs. Pierce approach us. I suddenly notice how very exhausted Angela looks. She has not said no, and she has not made that clicking sound with her mouth. She has not said yes, either.

Mrs. Pierce speaks to Angela briskly, telling her she must come home with them. Angela allows herself to be led away.

It is nearly dark now, and the air is filled with the sound of night insects. As I watch Angela walk away, I think of her little daughter and husband in Ndongo. I wonder if they still think of her every day, or if she has become a dim memory, lost forever to a foreign land.

Nineteen

THE LONG DAYS of summer shorten into fall. The tobacco harvest is finished and the large fragrant leaves hang in the barns to cure. Some nights are cool, and the insects keep quiet. Then it turns warm again, and the crickets and cicadas keep up their chirping nearly all night. I harvest the pumpkins from our garden and put them under my parents' bed. That's where they will stay until the dead of winter, when hot pumpkin soup will keep us fed.

The next time I see Angela, she is dressed in English clothing, with her arms properly hidden under long sleeves, though she still wears her indigo head wrap. Sometimes she chats in her own language with other Africans like Anthony and Isabella, but I am amazed at how quickly she is learning English.

An interesting thing happens to the music played in James Town in the evenings after work is done. The African men build drums in much the same way the natives build them, with deerskin stretched over a wooden frame.

The rhythms they play are quick and cheery and complicated, and when a group of musicians come together to play, the Africans join in. The African women dance, with their arms flying and hips keeping time. When we gather to listen and watch, I feel like I am flying as well. When I see Angela dance this way, I hope that just for a moment, she feels like she is back home in Ndongo.

We have another wedding with John Rolfe as the groom. He marries the Pierces' daughter, Jane. Angela helps Mrs. Pierce gather fall flowers to decorate the church.

Whenever Angela is not working, she is with Samuel. They go digging for clams and mussels together and go berry picking together. He even comes to help her with her work after he leaves the fields for the day. There is a sparkle in his eye whenever he talks about her.

I'm not the only one who has seen the sparkle. Cecily has not yet accepted a proposal of marriage because she has still been hoping that Samuel will choose her as his wife. She is furious about his new companion. One day I hear her gossiping at the well.

"She's *married*. And since she is a Christian, it must have been a Christian marriage, so she can't marry again unless her husband dies, and she'll never know if that happens. Not only that, she's a slave. What is he going to do, buy her?"

"She's . . . not really a slave." Mary speaks up hesitantly.

Good-hearted, level-headed Mary. "No one owns her because she escaped, so no one paid any money for her."

"Oh, you know what I mean. She's an *African*."

I take my buckets of water and hurry away. In whatever way I look at the situation, it confuses my mind and my heart. I just want Samuel to be happy, and he seems to be walking down a path that promises heartbreak.

• • •

As winter sets in, there is excitement in our family. With the corn harvest in storage and the tobacco harvest already shipped to England, my father finally has time to begin work on our homestead in Elizabeth City. Da and Samuel build a small shelter there so that they can travel down the river and stay for weeks, clearing the land and beginning to build our house. When they're gone, I miss them both, and I still don't like the idea of us moving. But when they come back each time so enthusiastic, with reports of their progress, I am happy for them, and some of their excitement rubs off on me.

Alice is becoming more of a help, and Katherine is growing strong. My father says he is building a house with not just one room like our cottage, but with actual "bed" rooms separate from the kitchen. This seems very strange to me, though I know this is how the fancier houses, like those of the noblemen, are built. Da says that when more brothers and sisters come along, we'll need more space.

At least during winter there are no new ships carrying colonists. We simply settle in to feed those of us who are here, stay warm, and as long as the ground is not frozen, bury those who die.

One Sunday afternoon in February, I go to see what Bermuda is doing. He has two piles of stones on the ground in front of him where he sits in the cold sunshine near his cottage. Next to him is an earthenware jar.

"What are you doing?" I ask.

"Counting ships," he answers.

I sit down in the dirt with him. "Are you pretending that those stones are ships?"

Bermuda shakes his head. "They represent the ships that have come to James Town since I started counting."

"When did you start counting?" I ask.

"About two years ago. Here, this pile is 1618," he says, and neatly separates six round stones. He points to a much larger pile. "These are 1619."

I widen my eyes. "No wonder it feels so crowded around here," I say. "Did you count them yet?"

"Fourteen," he says. "Fourteen ships with a thousand new colonists. My father says that's too many."

I feel slightly dizzy. I remember my dream of ships, and the feeling of too many ships coming to James Town.

"I wonder how many they'll send this year," I say.

Twenty

MY MOTHER SAYS springtime comes earlier in Virginia than it ever did in England. This makes me very glad I live in Virginia and not in England: I love springtime, and I would hate to have to wait for it to arrive. I am happy to dig and plant our garden and open up the shutters on our cottage that have been closed all winter. We have fresh turnip greens to eat, sprouting from the turnips we left in the ground during the cold months. Most of all I am happy that my father has to come home to begin work in the fields and leave our unfinished house in Elizabeth City to wait until next winter.

One day, just as the weather is warming up, a ship approaches. When the gangplank is lowered and the passengers unload, I am reminded of my dream of a shipload of women in white dresses. All of the passengers are young women dressed in upper-class finery. The gentlemen of the colony finally have their bride ship.

The women are not allowed to consort with servants

or other commoners. They have been sent for the gentle-men *only*.

The next few weeks are like watching a rooster-strutting contest. The gentlemen, in competition for the ninety or so young women, wear their swords, grease their mustaches, puff out their chests, don their finest clothes, and shine their shoes. Within a couple of weeks, the weddings begin. More than once an engagement has to be broken because it is discovered that the gentleman in question is already married to a wife in England. But as the honest men woo their mates and pay the Virginia Company for their brides with 150 pounds of choice to-bacco, Reverend Buck performs the wedding ceremonies.

There aren't nearly enough brides to go around, and so the order is sent back to England: send more suitable young women.

We also receive several shiploads of convicts. Ever since Governor Dale asked King James to please send us everyone in England who has been sentenced to death, we've been getting shiploads of convicted criminals.

Right from the beginning, Samuel reminded me that he himself was a convicted criminal, when he was eleven years old, sentenced to death for stealing his mother's locket back from a pawnshop. He told me not to be afraid of them, that they are not all bad people. And he's right. Many of them are thankful to be alive and throw them-selves into working hard for the colony. But when the summer flux hits, or when our stores run low and everyone is hungry, I've heard some of them complain that they should have chosen to be hanged in England rather than to come here.

Another shipload of London street children arrives. Then the *Treasurer* returns with more slaves to sell, and Captain Elfrith demands payment for Angela, his escaped "property." Angela is terrified that Captain Elfrith will take her on board the ship again, but Captain Pierce quietly pays the price, and the *Treasurer* sets sail away from James Town.

At supper one evening my father says, "Between the convicts, the Africans, the London street children, and all these indentured servants, we're becoming crowded with people who don't want to be here."

Katherine is on my lap, grabbing chunks of stew from the plate we're both sharing instead of letting me feed her. Alice is tapping her hands on the table, pretending she is playing an African drum.

"I didn't want to come here," my mother reminds him. "I was afraid of the journey across the ocean and I was afraid of the New World." She gives him a sweet smile. "But I'm glad I did come here."

"Oh, I remember you getting off the ship that day with your master and mistress," my father says. Alice stops tapping and listens, sensing a story coming on. "No one could believe they'd actually sent two women to

James Town. Conditions were terrible in those days. And then there you were, looking terrified, just fourteen years old." He leans toward her. "I didn't know if you were terrified of the place, or of being the one unmarried woman among all those lovesick men."

"Both!" my mother says.

I love hearing these stories about the time before I was born. Samuel was just a boy then. He has told me how he was worried about my mother, that she might starve that first winter if her selfish mistress didn't share enough rations with her. He says when my father won her heart and she had permission to marry, he thought, *Good, now she won't starve.*

Katherine splats her whole hand into our plate, ready to play now instead of eat. I clean her up with my napkin and set her on the floor. Alice reaches her spoon over to my plate and scoops up some of my stew. "Alice, what is wrong with your food?" I ask her.

"It's cold," she says.

"Well, mine is nice and warm because Katherine had her warm hands in it," I say.

"Good," says Alice, and she takes another spoonful of my stew.

"And now we have these three lovely daughters," my father says, beaming at each of us.

I sigh and pull Alice's plate over to my place so I can at least eat food that has not been mashed by baby hands.

Twenty-One

JUST AS THE hint of spring becomes a promise and it is time to plant pumpkin seeds in the garden, a ship arrives carrying more colonists, including a man named George Thorpe. The Virginia Company has set aside thousands of acres at Henrico to build a college where young Indian children can live and be taught the English ways of religion and culture. George Thorpe has been sent to carry out this plan, as the official "deputy for the college lands."

Mr. Thorpe wishes to meet with Chief Opechancanough in order to work with him on this plan. Samuel is asked to translate during the meeting.

I am hoeing weeds in the garden in late afternoon when Samuel returns from that first meeting. He looks worn-out.

I lean on my hoe as he approaches. "Are we soon to have a college filled with Indian children?" I ask, already knowing the answer.

Samuel shakes his head wearily. "Mr. Thorpe and Governor Yeardley and the Virginia Company officials, sitting in London—they are completely ignorant of the native ways. They think that the Powhatan people will send their children away like English nobles who send their children off to be educated."

"Was Mr. Thorpe angry when Chief Opechanca- nough said no?" I ask.

"He would never show it if he was angry," Samuel says. "They went round and round and round. Send the chil- dren; we will take excellent care of them. No, we do not send our children to live far from us. Our children are too precious to send away. But we will educate them and teach them to read and write, and then they will come home. No, we will not separate them from their families. I will send entire families to live with you if you would like."

"Did Mr. Thorpe like the idea of whole families com- ing?" I ask hopefully.

"No. Because he wants the Indian children to become more English. He doesn't want them to live in their own culture. So now he has all this land they have set aside— land that rightfully belongs to the natives, but the Com- pany says it's for the college—and money that has been donated to build and run the college, and not a single stu- dent." Samuel runs one hand through his hair.

I frown. "Isn't Governor Yeardley trading for the land? I mean, not just for the college land, but all the land we're expanding into—the homesteads for the ancients, and the new plantations for all the newcomers. Aren't the Indians being paid for it?"

Samuel lets out a groan. "No, they're not. The chief said there are many more of us than there used to be."

"Is Chief Opechancanough angry about the land being taken over?" I ask.

"He said that he and his brother Chief Opitchapam are both committed to peace between our people."

"That's good, right?" I ask.

"And Mr. Thorpe promised that he would make sure that our people treat all of his people with kindness and respect at all times," Samuel says.

I cock my head. "Then why do you look so worried?"

Samuel looks at me hard. "What happened to your knowing, Virginia? Can't you feel this one?"

I have been holding myself above it, keeping a thick veil between what my mind wants to think and what my heart would know if I only let it. On Samuel's suggestion, I allow an opening in the veil. For a moment, I sink into the knowing. Immediately, I feel it—the roiling cloud of Chief Opechancanough's rage, the fear for his people, the belief that the only way for his people to survive is to send the invaders away. I stagger at the power of it. "He wants us *gone*," I say softly.

"That is what I felt, too, behind all the agreeable

words," Samuel says. "But Mr. Thorpe will keep on giving gifts to Chief Opechancanough, and offering this education to their children, and being friendly and kind." He shrugs. "Maybe it will change him."

I nod slowly, wanting to believe that this change is possible.

Samuel squints toward the sun, turning red on the horizon. "And maybe it won't."

Twenty-Two

I HEAR THE scuffling and the shouts before I see the fight.

"Get him, he deserves it!"

"Beat the snot out of him and he'll never insult us again!"

The noise is coming from behind the church. When I come around the corner, I see who is being beaten up: Bermuda. There is a circle of children watching. It is Charles doing the beating. He grabs Bermuda by his shirt and punches him hard in the face. Bermuda's nose is streaming blood.

"Stop! Stop this *now!*" I shout.

Bermuda drops to his knees, his arms raised for protection. "You and your family are poor beggars and always will be." Charles spits out the words. Then he yanks Bermuda up and whacks the side of his head so hard, Bermuda goes sprawling onto the ground.

Rage overtakes me. I jump onto Charles's back, latch

one arm across his neck, and press *hard*. He lets out a guttural, strangled noise. He shakes his body violently, trying to throw me off. He punches my legs. But I am like a rabid dog. I do not let go. I will strangle him. I will *kill* him if I have to.

Charles stops moving. He hangs his arms down limp at his sides. I know this trick all too well. I keep my grip and growl into his ear, "You will not treat Bermuda like this again. And if you do, I will see to it that you die of the summer flux. Do you understand?"

Charles nods slightly. I press harder against his windpipe, unwilling to give him relief. Out of the corner of my eye, I see Bermuda scoot himself outside the circle. I see the other children watching, wide-eyed.

Suddenly Charles throws himself backward. In one swift motion, I am slammed to the ground. He lands his bulk on top of me and I hear a snap. Pain shoots through my right arm. I can't breathe. Charles rolls off me and stands. I stagger to my feet. He scowls at me.

"I will not punch a girl. Especially not a *witch*," he says. "Besides, I have everything I need now."

He walks away, and the children disperse with him.

I sit down in the dirt, hang my head, and grasp my throbbing arm. What was I *thinking*? How could I have been so careless, threatening the summer flux as if I know how to cast a spell?

Bermuda comes over and sits with me. Blood still

streams down his face and chin. His shirt is more dirt and blood than white cloth. "I'm sorry, Virginia," he says in a small voice.

"It's not your fault," I say.

"Why did he call you a witch?" Bermuda asks. "Do you know how to give someone the summer flux?"

"No," I say in a weak voice. Pain pulses in my arm. It feels as though my world is crashing down around me. I hold my head and begin to cry.

• • •

Samuel and Angela find us.

"Oh, no," Samuel says. He crouches down to look at the two of us, bleeding and muddy and miserable. "What on earth happened?"

Angela pulls a clean handkerchief out of her apron pocket and begins to clean Bermuda's face. "You lie down. Stop the blood," she orders him.

Bermuda does as he is told. "It was a fight," he says, his voice muffled behind the handkerchief Angela is holding to his nose.

"Ah," says Samuel, "and who won?"

I moan. The pain in my arm is making me feel faint and I don't care who won.

"We won," says Bermuda brightly. "They left." He tries to sit up, but blood trickles out of his nose, so Angela pushes him down again.

"Well, if winning a fight means getting the other fellow to stop beating you up, then I guess you won," says Samuel with more than a hint of sarcasm. Then he turns his attention to me. "Virginia, you look like you've seen a ghost. Are you all right?"

Darkness crowds the edges of my vision and I feel cold sweat break out on my forehead. "Home . . ." I say.

"Up you go," Samuel says, and he grasps my right arm to help me up.

Searing pain shoots through me. I scream. Everything goes black.

· · ·

When I come to, Samuel is carrying me. My left arm is draped over his shoulder and my right arm hangs loosely.

Samuel sees my open eyes. "Why didn't you tell us you were injured?" he asks. "We thought this was Bermuda's fight."

"It was Bermuda's fight," I mumble.

We arrive at my family's cottage. I shut my eyes tightly. My mother will be furious at me for getting hurt. And for what I said to Charles.

Samuel brings me inside and lays me down on the bed. Alice runs up to me. "Are you sick, Ginny?" she asks.

I shake my head. "I'm fine," I assure her. "Just a little bit hurt."

My mother has Katherine on one hip. She leaves the

stew pot she was stirring to come look at me. "What happened here?" she demands. Angela takes Katherine from her. My mother sits on the bed with me and smooths back my hair. I cringe. She will not be so compassionate when she hears about the threat I made.

Samuel tells her the story, obviously told to him by Bermuda while I was blacked out. He says Bermuda bragged to Charles and those other sons and daughters of gentlemen that his father was going to be a gentleman now that he and Bermuda's mother were being given land. My eyes grow wide. Bermuda handily started that fight himself. Samuel's story ends with, "She was trying to defend him and got herself hurt. I think her arm is broken."

My mother clicks her tongue. "Well now, while you were out getting into trouble, Bermuda, did you ever think that maybe Virginia has work she has to do? Did you? How am I to manage with two little ones and the cooking and the washing and sewing for the colony without Virginia to help me? Did you think of that when you decided to go bragging?"

I look through hazy vision at Bermuda. He hangs his head and sniffles. My mother is not finished. "The rules are different here, Bermuda. We common folk will be given land—you won't find that in England for sure. But don't go thinking—or saying—that it makes you any less a commoner. That is what you are, and that is what you will always be. Especially when it comes to *their* judgment of you." When she says *their*, it is with a flash of disdain.

"So, what do you expect me to do now, young man? Now that you've gone and gotten my daughter injured?" Mum looks as though she'll bore a hole through Bermuda's head with her stare. Even as woozy as I am, I know exactly what my mother is doing.

Bermuda looks up at her sheepishly. He shrugs. "I don't know," he says in a near whisper.

I close my eyes. "You're going to be working for her," I say.

"Exactly," Mum says. "And the first thing you can do is go fetch me water."

Bermuda doesn't dare object. He picks up a bucket and goes out immediately.

Mum then turns her attention to me. She moves expert, gentle fingers over my arm. When she hits the bad place, I groan. "All right," Mum says quietly. "It is broken. I'll have to set it."

She looks up to Samuel and Angela. "I'll need two thin boards and strips of rags . . . and whiskey if anyone has some to spare."

Though there is no wine or whiskey made in the colony—only ale—sometimes newcomers bring whiskey with them. I wonder what my mother needs it for. Maybe to clean my scratches and scrapes?

Angela sets Katherine down, and she and Samuel leave to gather things. My eyes fill with tears. "I'm so sorry, Mum," I say.

Alice pats my cheek. "Don't cry, Ginny," she says. "Be a big girl, don't cry."

Katherine toddles over and, imitating Alice's nice pats, she smacks my face.

"I'm sorry, too," Mum says. "But that Bermuda will learn a few things about taking care of babies and doing women's work."

"Mum, I did another bad thing," I say. My stomach twists. "I told Charles I would make sure he got the summer flux if he ever bothered Bermuda again."

Mum stiffens.

I continue, knowing I have to tell her the whole thing. "He called me a witch. He said he has everything he needs now to make a report to the governor."

Mum hangs her head and folds her hands. "Lord have mercy on us all."

I swallow hard. "I'm sorry, Mum. I was just so angry. I didn't think . . ."

"Virginia, I won't be able to save you," she says. There is both fear and determination in her voice. "If that boy accuses you, I won't be able to protect you. But for the sake of these two little ones, I will protect myself."

Her words jar me. I expected her to be angry, to reprimand me and punish me. I did not expect her to abandon me. I feel suddenly distant and alone, as if there is nowhere I belong anymore.

"Charles has lived through quite a few summers here," Mum is saying, trying to make me feel better. I probably look like I'm about to faint again. "Likely the summer flux won't bother him this summer either. It's best not to worry now."

But I am already withdrawing inside. If my own mother will not vow to love and protect me, then I am alone. I certainly can't tell my father about any of this. I begin to shiver and find I can't stop. Mum puts extra blankets over me, but it doesn't help.

Samuel, Angela, and Bermuda all arrive back at the same time. "We've got the boards and the rags, but no whiskey," Samuel says.

"And the water," says Bermuda.

"Good," Mum says. "She'll just have to do without the whiskey."

Do what without the whiskey? I wonder.

But before another thought can enter my head, my mother grasps my arm above and below the break. She pulls hard to set the bone in place. I feel a shriek of pain, then fall into darkness once more.

Twenty-Three

OVER THE NEXT few days, the pain in my arm subsides, but the pain in my heart does not. I am like an outsider, looking in at my family: my mother combing Alice's hair, my father kissing my mother before he leaves for the fields, Alice making Katherine laugh playing peekaboo. They are each loved. But I am *different.* There is something inside me that makes me strange, makes me unable to be loved and protected. In fact, it makes me a danger to all of them.

I spend my days with Bermuda, helping him with our household chores as best I can. He tries to learn how to change soiled diapers, but he can't keep hold of Katherine's feet and she keeps kicking into the mess and making things worse. Mum finally gives up and says she'll do it herself. Bermuda does not, however, get out of the job of washing soiled diapers in the river, along with the rest of our household laundry.

All the while I am waiting, expecting, dreading what Charles will find in his power to do to me. Every time I see him, he gives me a sly, knowing look, as if he is now in control, the predator, and I am his prey.

One evening, Samuel finds me in front of our cottage, closing our shutters for the night. "How is the arm?" he asks.

"Better each day," I say.

"I want to tell you something," he says. "Something I had to learn when I was your age."

I raise my eyebrows. "How to shoot a musket?" I ask.

He shakes his head. "About getting angry."

I pout. "Oh, that."

"Captain Smith and Reverend Hunt helped me learn that instead of letting my anger burst out punching and fighting, I could channel it. I could calm myself inside. Then I could make a better decision, one that wouldn't get me into so much trouble."

I sweep a cloud of gnats away with my one good arm. "How do you calm anger when it feels like a fire-breathing dragon?" I ask.

"First, I take a deep breath," he says. He thinks a moment. "You could imagine dumping a bucket of water on the dragon's fire," he suggests.

"If I had doused the dragon, I might still have jumped on Charles to protect Bermuda," I say. "But I wouldn't have threatened to give Charles the summer flux . . . and I wouldn't be waiting to see if he accuses me of being a witch."

• • •

Da is called away to help build houses at one of the outlying plantations. I don't want him to leave. He promises he'll only be gone for a little while, and to send Samuel to fetch him if I need him.

One day, soon after Da leaves, there is a knock on our door. It is Ensign Spence. He is a gentleman, one of the representatives to the House of Burgesses for James Town, and he also serves as assistant to Governor Yeardley. He brings the news I have been dreading: I have been accused. There will be a trial. In four days' time, at the next meeting of the General Assembly and the General Court, several cases will be heard, mine among them. I must be present to hear the testimony against me. My crime? Practicing witchcraft. The punishment? Public hanging.

When Ensign Spence leaves, I drop into a chair. Mum is pale and shaking. I look at her, wishing I could beg her for help, but I know I can't. We are both silent. Alice makes up for our lack of words.

"I don't like that man," she says. "I want him to stay away. Ginny, why are you sad now? What is a tri-yul?"

"Shush." Mum tries to quiet her.

But Alice keeps it up. "I want to know what a tri-yul is."

Katherine feels the tension and begins to cry. Mum picks her up. "Shush, Alice," she snaps. "You've upset the baby." Katherine cries even harder.

Alice. Katherine. Mum, for them. These are the people who can be protected now, not me. Alice. Katherine. They need their supper. I stand and walk to the fire. I watch my hand pick up the ladle and stir together the barley and peas of our loblolly. I will ladle it into their bowls. They will eat and be healthy. They will grow up strong and will not disappoint my mother the way I have. Once I am gone from the family, they will no longer be in danger.

That night I lie awake long after the others have gone to sleep. What will it be like to die, I wonder? Will I meet my grandmother? Will she take my hand and say, "I died a witch's death, too"? I shiver. I have only four days to wait to meet my fate.

. . .

Of course, there are no secrets in James Town. The next day Bermuda wants to know what is all this about a trial. Samuel comes by to tell me not to worry, that Governor Yeardley is squeamish about hangings and he certainly won't want to hang a young girl. Even Angela comes and embraces me.

"Remember," she says, holding my shoulders and looking into my eyes. "That day you find me? I was afraid

I die all alone in the forest. But you save me, give me apples and wet bread." We both laugh a little, remembering the soggy bread. "You have courage in here," she says, putting her hand on my heart. "Go inside, Virginia. Find who you are."

I nod, though I am not exactly sure how to do what she is telling me to do.

There are those who are not so kind. When I go to fetch water, the other girls at the well whisper to each other and look away. Even Reverend Buck, when he sees me picking up our rations, says, "This is a very serious charge, Virginia. I hope to God it's not true."

I want to shout, "Of course it's not true!" But I am too ashamed to speak. I hurry back to our cottage with our rations and slam our shutters closed.

"Why are you blocking out the light, Virginia?" my mother asks.

I choke back tears. "May I please work only in the cottage for the next few days?" I plead. "I can't go out there anymore."

Mum lays her hand against my cheek. I feel her fear. Fear for herself and what would happen to the little ones if she were gone. But especially fear for me. "Of course you can," she says. "But let's open the shutters so that I can see my sewing."

The next few days have a strange lightness about them. Mum and I both know, without saying it, that if all is lost, we must enjoy what is important now. We work side by side, grinding corn, kneading dough for our bread, keeping the candles burning and Katherine's diapers changed. We tell stories about the good things we remember. I take time to play with the girls, making them laugh with handy-dandy prickly-pandy. Finally, on the day before my trial, we send Samuel to get my father. We didn't want him to spend those days worrying from afar, but I don't want to die without seeing him again.

When Da arrives home, he is furious. "That boy and his family have done enough to us!" he shouts. I know he is remembering the child Mum lost because of her whipping. We all knew it was Charles's father who made the accusation against Mum, and Governor Dale who carried out his own form of justice.

Da lowers his voice to a growl. "I will sue him for defamation of character," he says. "He will pay."

Da points one finger at me. "You were careless, Virginia. You don't deserve this, but *you were careless*." He paces. I have never seen him this angry.

"I'm sorry, Da," I say.

He raises his hand as if he will strike me. I cower. Then he grabs his own hand as though he is shocked at what he almost did.

"They will give us land because we are ancients," he says, still seething. "But make no mistake. We are still commoners, and the gentlemen and nobles still hold the power." He narrows his eyes at me. "Do not *ever* speak to your betters that way again. Do you understand?"

I nod quickly, not even daring to say *I'm sorry* again.

Da's confidence buoys me. He is talking as if I have many years to follow his advice, as though he will have plenty of time to sue for defamation of character after Charles loses this case against me.

When we all bed down on this last night before my trial, I have hope.

Alice pats my hand. "Have fun at the tri-yul tomorrow, Ginny," she says. Mum has told her that a trial is where people come together to talk and discuss things, and she is satisfied with that explanation despite all of the emotions flying around.

I kiss Alice's forehead. "Thank you," I say.

But during the night I awaken to the sound of muffled sobs, and my parents talking in tight voices. "What if they take her from us? What if there is nothing we can do to prevent them from hanging her?"

"I know, John. I have not stopped praying, not for a moment."

"Pray for a miracle. . . ."

Then all I hear is both of them weeping.

Fear clutches me again with icy fingers. I lie awake until dawn.

• • •

Samuel breezes in without knocking, as he always does. "Come on, Ginny," he says. "Let's go get this over with." He nods to my parents. "I'll take her so you two can get to work. I'll have her back by noon." And before anyone can ask any questions, he whisks me out the door.

I have to trot to keep up with Samuel's long strides. "Your parents look awful," he says. He glances at me. "So do you."

"Thanks," I say.

"I'm telling you, Governor Yeardley does not like hangings or whippings. How many have we had since he took office?"

I don't want to think about this, so I don't answer.

We arrive at the church, where the General Assembly meeting has already begun. They are discussing how much to tax the colonists to pay themselves for the time they spend meeting.

"The trials will come a little later," says Samuel, and he bids me sit next to him under a tree outside the church entrance. A man, dressed in the shabby clothing of an indentured servant, paces back and forth at the church entrance. He is being guarded by a man with a musket. I figure they are waiting for a trial as well.

"How is your arm?" Samuel asks.

I lift my arm, still in its splint. "Better," I say. "But it still hurts, and it's bent a little funny." A group of young men walk by, on their way to the fields. "Don't you need to get to work?" I ask.

"Yes," he says. "My trial will be next. Samuel Collier, charged with skipping a day of labor in the tobacco fields. Twenty lashes!"

"That's not funny," I say. "Da says we're still commoners and if the gentlemen and nobles want to use their power over us, they will."

"Do you want me to leave you and go to work?" he asks.

I shake my head quickly.

"Then let me deal with the consequences," he says.

The voices inside the church drone on. I wish they would hurry up and get to the trials. Gnats buzz around my head and I begin to feel sleepy. After all, I hardly slept last night. I lay my head back against the tree.

"You can go to sleep, Ginny," Samuel says. "I'll listen for when your case is called."

Twenty-Four

I MUST HAVE fallen sound asleep, because when the commotion awakens me, I am lying on my side on the ground. I sit up quickly. The indentured servant we saw earlier is being led away, his hands tied behind his back. He is shouting,

"I didn't steal anything!" he cries. "It was food he owed me! He's starving me so I will die and he won't have to pay me my freedom dues. He is a liar!"

But no one is listening to him. The council members march after him as he is led away.

"Ginny, let's go home," Samuel says. "The meeting is over for the day."

"Where are they going?" I ask. I am groggy, and it feels as though I am in a dream.

"Never mind," Samuel says.

One look at him tells me something is very wrong. "What are they doing?" I demand.

Samuel hesitates. "He works for one of the nobles on a plantation. . . ." he begins, but then stops.

My mind fills in the rest. I know how the most powerful men treat their servants as though they are not even human. To avoid paying them their freedom dues—corn, clothing, and a bit of money—at the end of their indenture, they often simply stop feeding them so that they die conveniently. This master apparently found a quicker way to be rid of his servant. "His master accused him of stealing," I say. "So now he will be hung?"

Samuel shakes his head. "Whipped," he says. But we both know that severe whippings can, and have, killed quite a few servants. "Let's get you home," Samuel says.

"I hate them!" I cry. "They treat us worse than dogs!"

I jump to my feet and run. I want *out*—out into the forest, where I will be safe from the power-wielding gentlemen and nobles. Samuel catches up and grabs me, but I kick him and he lets go.

A crowd is gathering around the whipping post.

"Ginny, don't," Samuel calls after me.

At the fort gate, two guards step out in front of me, their muskets held sideways, blocking my way. Extra security for trial day. Samuel is right behind me. "She's with me," he says to the guards. "I'll take her home now."

"Leaving the fort to avoid justice?" one of the guards asks. "Maybe you want to be next on the whipping post?"

"She has not set foot outside the gates," Samuel snaps.

"We'll take care of her," the other guard says.

In an instant, they grab me, one under each arm. I cry out in pain.

"Careful of her arm!" Samuel shouts.

My feet scarcely touch the ground as they whisk me past the crowd at the whipping post. The indentured servant is being tied to it. I choke on bile that churns up from my stomach.

"We don't want you to end up there simply because you ran away," one of the guards says.

We pass the chicken coop and they drag me into the storehouse. Are they going to lock me up with the barrels of grain and baskets of dried oysters? They take me down the earthen steps into the cellar. There is a wooden partition and a door. When they open the door, I see a chamber pot, a rough blanket in a heap, and the remains of a fire on the floor.

"You'll be safe here till morning," one guard says, and they shove me in.

When the door closes behind me, I can see nothing. I hear a board being set across the door to lock me in. It is cold and damp, and smells of urine. I slump onto the floor. I am thirsty. And hungry.

I lean my head onto my bent knees and close my eyes. I am weary. Weary of the fear, weary of trying to do what my parents want from me and never quite being able to. I am weary of feeling as though my sisters are in danger because of me. I let out a long, shaky breath. Maybe it would be all for the best. I imagine the prickly rope of the noose being tightened around my neck. I imagine being pushed off the gallows platform, the rope snapping my neck, and all of my weariness and fear being over.

A chill creeps up my back in the damp. I feel around for the blanket and touch its roughness. I pull it across my shoulders. Immediately I feel something crawl across my face. I swat at it but I am too late. There is a pinprick of a sting, and then a growing fire.

I throw the blanket far from me, but the damage has been done. The burning pain spreads across my face, and I feel the swelling begin. It must have been a spider.

Soon I feel fever overtake me. I shiver with chills, and my stomach roils in pain. My mind feels hazy, but I recognize the symptoms of a poisonous spider bite—one of those shiny black spiders with the red hourglass on its back.

I am so very thirsty. I rock back and forth, my body consumed with pain, chills, and thirst. I begin to pray, to find comfort in the familiar words I've learned in church. "Our Father, who art in heaven . . ." When I am done with the prayers I know, I keep on whispering, talking to God in my own words. "I never meant to do anything wrong," I tell Him. "I have tried to obey my parents." I sigh, thinking of how my mother told me to kill the knowing inside me, and how I failed. "I just hope that

You will let me into heaven even if I die as a criminal." I shiver with the fever. I hug my knees and try to curl into a ball to get warm. As I sit huddled against the dirt wall, one memory comes to me as clearly as if it is happening again: Angela holding me by the shoulders, then touching my heart, and her words: "Go inside, Virginia. Find who you are."

Angela has been here, huddled, sick, thirsty, hungry, and miserable. She has told me about how she was chained with hundreds of other slaves on the passage from Africa across the ocean. She told me how they lay in their own filth and blood and vomit, unable to move because of the chains, how so many died of sickness and despair. She also told me how, in that very dark place, deep inside her, she found the light of her own soul to be burning brightly.

Is there a light within me as well? I shut my eyes tightly, as if I am squinting to look into my soul. *Go inside, Virginia. Find who you are. . . .*

I groan. I see no light at all. What I see is a girl who has tried to do the right thing and has ended up in a dungeon with poisonous spiders, awaiting execution. What I see is a girl who tried to do what her parents wanted and never could.

"Dear God, is there no light in me?" I cry out. Tears press behind my eyes and I let them fall. The words float to me again, insistent, as if I have not yet really heard them: *Go inside, Virginia. Find who you are.*

Suddenly a thought stops my tears. I only know who I am supposed to be, which is who I have failed to be. There has never been any room for knowing who I might be, behind all the things I have been trying to be. *Let us start from the begining.* These words float to me, and I don't even question where they come from.

"I am Virginia Laydon," I say. "Daughter of—" But I stop myself. My parents are not who I am. Let me begin with just *me.* "I am Virginia," I say. "I love the forest, the life I feel in the trees and plants, rocks and earth. I love my family, my sisters and Mum and Da and Samuel. I love my friends, Bermuda and Angela. I—" I hesitate to say what is in me to say next. But this is all I have, a few hours to find the light of my soul before it is consecrated to God. "I love the knowing. It has been given to me by God; it is what led me to find Angela and save her life. It is a good thing. I love it."

There. I said it. And now there is something more for me to say that does not fit with who I am "supposed" to be. "I am Virginia, and I love my anger!" I say it loudly, feeling the freedom of claiming it. "My anger flashes up and helps me protect the people I love, like Bermuda, or my sisters." I hesitate. "It doesn't always make me say or do the right thing," I say sheepishly. "But it is part of who I am.

"I am Virginia," I continue. "I am honest. I am faithful. I work hard. I am cheerful when I can be. I am fierce when I have to be. I love all of this about myself."

Something is lifting. My face still burns, I am still shivering with fever, and my stomach still twists with pain and nausea. The misery is not lifting from my body, but something is lifting from my spirit. I close my eyes and look inside myself. I see a faint light. It begins at my heart. "I am Virginia," I whisper. "I am the way God made me. I love . . ."

As I say the word "love," the light inside me brightens.

"I am the way God made me." I say it again. "And I love who I am!"

The light spreads and fills me. I laugh out loud. I have found the light of my soul.

"Thank you, thank you, thank you," I say. No one can take this light away from me, not with threats or blows, not with a whipping or even the gallows. It is mine.

Twenty-Five

WHEN THE GUARDS come to let me out in the morning, I can barely walk. Through the night, pain and stiffness has spread into my limbs. I am still shivering, and hunger and thirst have made me weak. One eye is swollen nearly shut, and my lips are dry and cracked. I stumble and fall on the steps leading up from my dungeon. The guards help me up and I smile at them. As I do, I feel my lips crack, and blood seeps down my chin.

"What happened to her?" one guard asks.

"It's those blasted spiders," the other answers. "Though she looks worse than most."

It somehow gives me satisfaction to know that my body looks as bad as it feels. It makes the contrast even greater, because my spirit is as light as sunshine. There is nothing that can scare me today. Nothing.

The guards lead me across the fort to the church. It seems my trial is about to get under way. The men of the General Court look down at their papers, glance at me, and frown. I see several of them whispering among themselves. Light glints in through the church windows, the same way it does during church services. Today, these men will judge me. But I know that only my heavenly Father is my real judge.

Charles sits on a bench, staring straight ahead. I can't read his expression. It is tempting to bump into him as the guards lead me past him so that one touch will tell me what he is thinking. I am curious. Will he rejoice if he is responsible for the death of someone he knows full well is innocent? Or did the whipping yesterday make him reconsider?

One guard motions for me to have a seat on an empty bench. Governor Yeardley sits where Reverend Buck normally stands. He calls the guard over. "Did someone beat her?" he demands.

"No!" the guard objects. "We just put her in the store-house cellar. It's got spiders."

Governor Yeardley shakes his head and clears his throat. "The proceedings of the General Court will begin," he says.

I am calm. There is nothing that can be said against me that will be true, except that I made empty threats in anger. If these men judge me guilty, it will be based on lies.

Ensign Spence reads from a written document. It is Charles's testimony against me. In a loud, booming voice, he reads, "The accused came into his room at night, sat on him, and tried to strangle him. She said she would use an evil spell to make him fall ill with the summer flux and die. She turned into a black cat and disappeared through the keyhole of his chamber door."

By now I am staring at Charles with my mouth hanging open. He continues to look straight ahead, but he seems slightly worried. Maybe his fantastical story doesn't sound quite so convincing to him now that it is being read in a court of law.

Ensign Spence addresses me. "Is it true that you sat on him and tried to strangle him?"

I clear my throat. "I did strangle him a bit," I begin. There is mumbling among the council members. "But that didn't happen in his chamber. It happened outside in the dirt, with a group of children watching, the day of the fight."

"What fight?" Ensign Spence asks.

I show him my splint. "The one where he broke my arm. That was the day he was beating up my friend, so I—"

Ensign Spence interrupts me. "The night you entered his chamber, what happened then?"

"I was never in his chamber," I say simply.

He looks down at his papers. "What about the night you turned into a black cat and went through his key-hole?"

I blink. "I have always been a girl, sir. I have never been anything else."

There is laughter among the council members.

Ensign Spence reads his papers again. He is beginning to sound annoyed. "Did you or did you not threaten him with an evil spell to give him the summer flux?"

My throat tightens. I speak slowly. "I did not threaten him with an evil spell, sir. I know nothing of these things."

"Yes, she did!" It is Charles, on his feet now. "She said she would cast a spell on me and make me sick and die, the same way her mother put an evil spell on my mum and then my da and made them die!"

I feel a strange thing: compassion for Charles. He thinks my mum took both his parents away from him. I want to say, *She would never do that to you!*

"Sit down," Ensign Spence orders Charles.

I am ready to confess that I did threaten to make sure he got the summer flux, but that I only said it because I was so angry, and I had no way to make it happen. I suck in my breath, ready to blurt it all out. But Governor Yeardley slams down his gavel.

"This is a children's quarrel. Send these children home and stop wasting this court's time. The defendant is innocent and this case is over. Now, let us get on with more important business."

Charles is ushered out of the church and I limp slowly

toward the doors. "The doctor should be seen for that spider bite," Governor Yeardley says. It is strange to have the governor address me personally.

"I will go home to my mother, sir," I say. I think to add, *She will heal me with herbs*, but decide I'd better not bring up anything that might be associated with witch-craft.

As I step outside, Alice runs to me and hugs me around the waist. I look up to see Mum holding Katherine on one hip, looking devastated with worry.

"I'm fine, Mum," I say. Then, knowing my face must still look awful, I add, "It's just a spider bite."

"And the trial?" she asks. I can see she is holding back an ocean of tears.

I grin and feel my lips crack further. "The trial has a happy ending. Please let's go home and get me a drink of water, and then I will tell you about it."

Katherine has been staring at me.

"Does my face look funny?" I ask her.

She nods solemnly.

"She just got bit by a spider," Alice says. "She's going to be fine."

I ruffle Alice's hair. "You are so right," I tell her. "I'm going to be just fine."

At home Mum makes a poultice of herbs and spreads it on my swollen face. She mixes together tallow and melted beeswax, and while it is still warm, spreads it on my cracked lips. Then she makes me hot tea from more herbs and warms some porridge for me to eat. In a short time, I feel the poison leaving my body, and I am able to move without my arms and legs hurting.

Samuel and Da come back from their work, and even Bermuda comes to hear about my trial. I tell the story, and when I get to the part about me becoming a black cat, Alice bursts out laughing. Soon Katherine is giggling too, and then everyone joins in. The words that were so shocking and threatening in front of the General Court have now become a hilarious joke.

"That boy doesn't know up from down," Da says. "I won't even bother to sue him for defamation of character. Better to put all of this behind us."

I am relieved. I do not want to spend any more time in court.

• • •

I am walking to the well with the yoke across my shoulders and both buckets hanging. It is a sweltering summer day. As I approach the well, I see there are three boys and a commotion is going on. One of the boys is Charles, and the other two I have seen around.

"I didn't drop it on purpose," Charles snaps.

"No, you didn't drop it—you threw it!"

"My da gave me that knife." The smaller of the two boys is near tears.

"I'll get it out," Charles says with annoyance.

"How? It's sunk."

They lower the bucket, and Charles leans into the well, his whole upper body inside the narrow stone walls.

This is an opportunity I do not want to miss. I take my last few steps at a trot. I hold the yoke steady with my hands, swing the left end of the yoke back, and then throw it forward, smacking it, with its bucket, squarely into Charles's derriere.

He yelps, grabs his behind, and pulls his head out of the well.

The other two boys erupt in laughter.

"That was for lying about me," I say.

"Whoa, Charles, you got this pretty girl mad at you," one of the boys says.

"She is *not* a pretty girl." Charles spits out the words. He is beyond furious.

"Oh yes, she is," says the other boy.

My cheeks flush, but I keep my focus on Charles. "Don't ever lie about me again," I say.

There is no hope of getting water now, so I turn and head back home. As I walk away I hear the boys teasing Charles about his "sweetheart." From now on if he pays me any attention at all, they will think it is because he is sweet on me rather than because he despises me. My guess is, he will do his best to avoid me.

Twenty-Six

I WANT TO like Mr. George Thorpe. I want to believe that it is from a good place in his heart that he is planning this college for the Indian children. I've heard that one of the boys who went to England with Pocahontas ended up living with Mr. Thorpe there, and he adopted him as his own son. He taught the boy to read. He read the Bible, became a Christian, and was baptized with the Christian name Georgius. When Georgius died of English disease, Mr. Thorpe paid to have him buried properly in a church graveyard.

People are saying that now Mr. Thorpe wants to build this school in memory of Georgius, whom he loved so much. But why would he think that taking children away from their loving families is a good thing?

Mr. Thorpe says that our ways are better than native ways, and that their children should learn our ways. The children's parents don't agree, and Mr. Thorpe does not have a single student. But still, I have tried to understand him and like him. Then, one day, Mr. Thorpe does something that makes me hate him.

Since no one is allowed to write back to England about how hungry we are sometimes here, and since the Virginia Company advertises that our colony has "All the Deer, Fish, and Fowl you can eat," it's no wonder some noblemen arrive with their great mastiff dogs in tow. The dogs are supposed to help with the hunting, and they do, but I think they easily eat more than they help, since they are the size of small horses. A lot of people don't like them because they say in winter, servants die of starvation while the noblemen's dogs are well fed.

We have two mastiffs that live near us in James Town fort, Ulysses and Sheba. Katherine and Alice love them, and always want to pet them even though they have to reach *up* to pat these giants on the head. Ulysses and Sheba are gentle giants—unless they are provoked.

It is a cloudy day, threatening rain. I am walking with Alice and Katherine, holding their hands, heading to the chicken coop to pick up our ration of eggs. The girls spy Sheba and Ulysses and ask if they can go pet them.

But there is shouting and arguing. The dogs' master is red-faced, sputtering. Another man is waving his arms and yelling something about an unfair price. People are gathered, watching—some are settlers and some are the natives who live among us.

Suddenly, the angry man takes a menacing step forward.

Sheba lowers her head and bares her teeth. Ulysses growls, ready to spring. The shouting man is suddenly still. Either of these dogs could kill him with a single bite to the neck. The man backs up slowly, terrified.

My sisters have no sense. They just see the dogs and want to pet them *now*. They both wriggle their hands out of my grasp and go running, ducking between the onlookers. I rush after them, but people are in my way.

I'm too late. I watch with horror as Alice reaches toward Ulysses, and Katherine holds both hands up to Sheba. I scream, "No!"

The next thing I see is Ulysses licking Alice's face. Sheba lifts a paw to shake hands with Katherine and knocks her over. Both girls are giggling.

I am trembling when I get to them. I grasp them each by the arm and drag them away. "Those dogs were angry," I tell them sternly. "You can't play with them until they calm down."

Alice gives me a pout. "They're not angry, they're nice," she says.

As people disperse to go about their business, I hear muttering about the "bad dogs" or the "good dogs." Everybody has an opinion.

It is two days later that Mr. George Thorpe does the horrible thing. He hears that several of the native men who watched the incident are now afraid of Sheba and Ulysses. Mr. Thorpe is doing everything he can to convince the natives to send their children to his college. Does he really think that his next despicable act will sway anyone?

Mr. Thorpe holds a public hanging. The criminals? Sheba and Ulysses. They are hung for no other crime than love for their master. Of course, we do not go to watch. Katherine and Alice are heartbroken enough when we tell them that Sheba and Ulysses have died and gone to heaven. And I hope that if Mr. Thorpe somehow, someday, makes his way to heaven, that those two beautiful dogs bite him as soon as he arrives.

• • •

I carry a basket, on my way to pick blackberries, hoping to get there before the birds or the other settlers have eaten all the ripe ones. A thunderstorm has just swept through and the air feels scrubbed clean and shiny with sunlight.

I see the blackberry brambles from a distance. I also see that someone is already there picking. I hurry to get there more quickly, but when I am closer, I see that it is Samuel and Angela. I raise my hand, ready to call out a greeting, but I stop. Samuel picks a berry, then leans in close to Angela and slips the berry into her mouth. She tips her head up and he kisses her lips.

I wish I could feel happy, watching them in love. But all I feel is sadness, knowing that they will never be allowed to marry. Samuel suddenly thinks to look around and sees me. "So, we've been caught by the James Town guard, have we?" he calls out cheerily.

I march down the path to them, my basket swinging. When I get to them, all I can think of to say is "I won't tell anyone."

"Oh, I don't think it's any big secret," Samuel says.

Angela is flustered, embarrassed. I want to tell her it's all right, that I'm not judging her for being a married woman in love with someone else. How can she keep her heart closed when she knows she will never see her husband again?

"I should go," she says, and picks up her own basket, empty of berries.

"We'll help you fill your basket so you don't get into trouble," I say quickly, and take her basket from her.

We begin to pick, silently at first. But I am growing angrier by the second. Finally, I blurt out, "It's not fair!"

They both look at me.

"God makes rules, and men make rules, and when men make rules that make it impossible to follow God's rules, then who is to blame?!" I fix Angela with a stare. "*Not* you." I point at her. "But they will blame you." My voice catches in my throat. "They will say what you are doing is wrong." I turn to Samuel. "And what if they say you have committed a crime? What if they decide to whip you, or hang you?" I wipe tears away with my fist.

Samuel puts an arm around me. "I have a plan," he tells me. "It will be all right, Ginny."

I shake my head hard. "There is no plan that can fix this," I say. "She is married, and someone's property, and no one will give you permission to marry."

Angela quietly slips away. Samuel pulls me over to a fallen log and bids me to sit down with him.

"Just listen. Will you listen?" he asks.

I nod.

"Problem number one, she is a slave belonging to Captain and Mrs. Pierce. I have land now. I can grow tobacco, ship it back to England for a profit, and earn the money to buy her."

I purse my lips. I'd never thought of him *actually* buying her.

"I figure it will take me two years to earn enough for her purchase price," Samuel continues. "Even if I have to go hungry, I'll skip the corn and plant every inch of my land in tobacco to make the most profit."

I roll my eyes. "You won't go hungry, because my mother will feed you."

"Fair enough," he says.

"But you want to marry her, not own her," I say. "She is married and she is a Christian, so it is a Christian marriage. You'll never know if her husband dies, so she will never be free to marry again."

"What if it was not a Christian marriage?" he asks. "What if she was baptized after she was wed? John Rolfe was allowed to marry Pocahontas even though she was already married, because her marriage to Kocoum did not count in the eyes of the church."

"Are you sure she was wed before she was baptized?" I ask.

"Are you sure she wasn't?" he asks.

I blink at him. Angela was kidnapped by Portuguese slave traders, then stolen by English pirates, then sold. No one here knows anything about how her wedding ceremony was performed. It is a secret that will go with her to the grave, and that she can discuss with her Maker when the time comes.

I lift my face up to the sun. "I like your plan, Samuel Collier," I say. "I like it very much."

• • •

Samuel must have confided his plan to some of his friends, who in turn told it to their friends, because soon Samuel and Angela are the topic of gossip all over the fort. People normally go silent when they see me or anyone from my family, but one day at the well, I find Cecily and her friend Ester. They ignore me and keep on gossiping.

"So, he'll buy her and own her. How romantic," Cecily says.

Ester makes a face.

"And what if they do marry?" Cecily continues. "Their children will be *mongrels*."

I slam my water buckets to the ground, nearly breaking them.

Cecily looks at me, startled. Then she goes back to calmly turning the crank on the well. "What's the matter, Virginia?" she says. "Don't you like hearing the truth?"

What I want to do is punch her. Instead, my mind flashes back to my fight with Charles, and my talk with Samuel. I take a deep breath. In my mind's eye, I see myself pulling up a bucket of water and tossing it over the head of my fire-breathing dragon anger. Only then do I speak.

"I heard you are betrothed, are you not, Cecily?" I ask sweetly.

"Yes, to William," she says.

"You wouldn't want him to think you're still pining away after Samuel, would you? I mean, if someone told William how much you still talk about Samuel, that might make him angry, don't you think?"

Cecily's face turns its signature bright red. She snatches her bucket off the hook. "I am *not* jealous, you little wench," she snaps.

"I usually see William at the tar pits when I visit my friend Bermuda," I say.

She narrows her eyes at me. "Don't you dare say a

word to him!"

"Maybe you should talk less if you don't want your words to reach William," I say.

I hook one of my buckets to the rope and let it down into the well. I hum and focus on my work.

"Come on, let's go," Cecily says. She pulls on Ester's arm.

"I haven't fetched my water yet," Ester objects. But Cecily drags her away.

I hum louder, one of the Irish tunes the musicians play, as I crank up my full bucket of water.

Twenty-Seven

SUMMER PASSES AND Charles does not die of the summer flux. It is more evidence of my innocence because he certainly made me angry enough to curse him if I possibly could have.

Da can hardly wait for the tobacco harvest to be over so that he and Samuel can go back to Elizabeth City to work on clearing the land and building our houses. As he prepares to leave, Katherine and Alice set up whining and crying that they don't want him to go.

"I'm building us a nice house," he promises them.

"I don't want a nice house," Alice wails. "I want you to stay here in this house."

"I have to clear our land for our farm," Da says patiently.

"No fawm!" Katherine cries.

My mother and I look at each other over their heads. The little girls are doing what we wish we could do: cling to my father and beg him not to leave us.

My father picks up his weeping daughters and sets one on each knee.

"Look," he says loudly, startling them into silence. "Look at me. Where am I, Alice?" he asks.

"Right here," she says, and sniffs.

"Katherine, where is your da?"

"Here." She points to his chest.

"Yes, I'm right here with you. So, stop crying."

Alice lowers her face to the sleeve of his shirt and wipes her snotty nose on it. Da's lecture seems to have satisfied them, because soon they are playing on the floor with their rag dolls, and Da is free to continue packing.

The next day, Da and Samuel leave for Elizabeth City while the girls are napping.

• • •

It begins almost as soon as my father leaves. I wake up with it in the morning and feel it as I lie down to go to sleep at night: dread. During the day when I am busy, the feeling fades into the background. But whenever I am quiet, it is there waiting for me, like a menacing storm in the distance, letting me know that somehow, some way, we are in danger.

If only Samuel were here, I'd be able to talk to him about it. I don't want to worry my mother by telling her about this dread, or by admitting to her that the knowing is alive and well in me. I keep an extra-close watch on the girls whenever I am out of the house with them, and I refuse to take Alice with me outside the fort no matter how hard she begs.

One day in late January the weather turns warm as springtime. "If we had no calendar, I would think it was time to plant," my mother says. We open the shutters, and the low winter sun streams into our cottage. "Go take Alice with you to fetch wash water from the river," my mother tells me.

Katherine is sleeping, Alice has refused to nap, and I know my mother wants some peaceful time to work on her sewing. I can't object. I can't tell her I'm worried that there might be something out there to harm us. All I can do is agree and lift the yoke with buckets to my shoulders.

It's so warm we don't even bother to wrap our feet in rags. Alice chatters all the way to the river. Is it springtime yet? Is Da coming home tomorrow? If it's still winter, then why is it so warm? When is Da coming home? When will it be spring? Why not now?

I answer her questions patiently, all the while glancing around us to make sure there is nothing out of the ordinary. At the river, I lower the yoke from my shoulders. The air is warm, but the water is frigid, so when I wade in to dunk my buckets, my feet hurt with cold.

Alice plays on the shore, jumping from rock to rock. I sit down near her to thaw my frozen feet in the sun. Alice is so happy to finally be out, it would be a shame to rush her back to our cottage. She begins to gather small stones and arrange them in a pile. *We'll stay just a little while longer*, I tell myself. Mum will be glad for the quiet time.

I look out across the river at the line of trees on the other shore, and the gap in the trees where our laborers have felled them to clear land for a new plantation. I wonder what it must have looked like when Samuel and my father arrived on those first ships, when all the trees still stood proud and tall.

Now Alice is using her four-and-a-half-year-old strength to lift and move big rocks. *Good*, I think, *maybe she'll get tired and take a nap after all.* The warmth and sun are making me sleepy, so I fold up my knees, rest my arms and head on them, and close my eyes.

The next thing I hear is Alice's scream. I jump to my feet. The snake slithers away. There are two small holes on Alice's leg already dripping blood. She is wailing in pain.

I whisk her into my arms and run, up the bank, past the fort watchmen, and crash into our cottage. "Snake. Maybe a cottonmouth, maybe a copperhead. I don't know," I cry. "I thought they were all sleeping! It's winter!"

Mum grabs Alice and lays her on the bed. "Hold her," she orders.

While I hold down a screaming Alice, Mum sucks the blood and poison out of her wound, spitting it onto our dirt floor.

I am shaking. It is my fault. A snakebite can kill a grown man, and much more easily a small child. Why didn't I watch her better? She must have lifted a rock off a snake's hibernation den and awakened it. Why did I not tell my mother about the feeling of dread? Why didn't I just admit that the knowing had given me a warning, and refuse to take Alice outside the fort? I protected myself instead of protecting Alice.

"I'm so sorry. I'm so sorry," I say it over and over.

Mum is all business. "Bring me tobacco," she demands. Because there were no copperheads or cottonmouths in London, her knowledge of how to treat New World snakebites comes from the Powhatans. Mum chews on the dried tobacco leaves, then puts the chewed-up wad onto Alice's leg. "This will draw out more of the poison," she says.

Poison. When she speaks the word, I get a strong jolt of the knowing. Poison is the threat. Poison is what I have been dreading. But not from this sleepy snake—he was only the messenger.

I am suddenly calm. I know that Alice will heal. I place my hands firmly on Alice's head. She has stopped screaming and is merely whimpering. "You're going to be fine," I tell her. "Let Mum do what she needs to do and you'll be well soon."

My mother glances at me. She is wondering how I

know, afraid that it is the knowing, wanting it to be the knowing so that she can be assured of the truth of what I have said. "Don't worry about Alice, Mum," I say, answering her unasked questions. "Don't worry about me, either." I am on my own now, anyway—she no longer needs to protect me.

She gives me a crooked, tentative smile. She holds the tobacco against Alice's leg as Alice continues to whimper.

Katherine, who slept through the loudest parts, now sits up in bed. "Alice hurt?" she asks.

"Yes," I say, "but Mum knows what to do, and she'll be up to play with you very soon."

The rest of the day Alice refuses to eat. She says her stomach feels bad. I remember touching the purple coneflowers when I was a small child and knowing that they would be good for snakebites. My mother is doubtful of it, but I make tea from our dried purple coneflowers and give it to Alice to drink. She says it makes her stomach feel a little better.

Alice is weak and stays lying in bed. Her foot and ankle swell up and the skin around the bite turns deep purple. It is a frightful sight, but I am confident in the knowing that she will survive this.

News of Alice's snakebite travels fast through the colony and soon we have visitors. Jane is the first to arrive. She and Mum discuss treatment and decide to make a poultice of burdock root to further draw out the poison and help with healing. I sprinkle a little dried purple cone-flower into the poultice.

Jane also gives us an egg from her rations. "Feed this to her when she feels good enough to eat," she tells my mother. It is well known that healthy people survive these bites. It's the ones that are sickly or half starved that die. "You keep these girls well fed with your garden," Jane says, trying to dispel my mother's worry. "And Alice is strong."

Alice doesn't look strong, lying there with glassy eyes and her swollen, half-purple leg, still crying sometimes because of the pain.

Bermuda comes in the evening, carrying the yoke and water buckets I left lying at the river. "I heard," he says. He looks worried and scared, and doesn't stay long.

Next to arrive is Angela, with an earthenware pot of baked apples, sent by Mrs. Pierce. It smells wonderful, and Alice actually sits up and eats a little of it.

"Do you want to hear a story?" Angela asks.

Alice nods. "Tell about Anansi," she says.

Katherine climbs into my lap and Angela begins. "Anansi was a spider. A *very* tricky spider. But he also a greedy spider." She makes a grabbing motion with one hand to show how greedy Anansi was. "One day he went to Sun God and said, 'You have all wisdom in the world. I want you to give it to me.' So, Sun God put all wisdom into a calabash and gave it to Anansi."

Alice's eyes are bright as she listens. Katherine sits quite still in my lap. "Anansi was very happy with calabash full of wisdom. He was smartest in the world now! But one day he said, what if someone tries to take my wisdom? Then I will not be smartest in the world. I must hide the calabash."

Angela holds out her arms as if she is Anansi the spider, holding a big pot of wisdom. "So, he carried the calabash to a tall tree, full of thorns. 'I hide the calabash in top of this tree,' he said. But first he has to climb the tree."

Angela stands and acts out Anansi trying to climb while holding the pot in front of him. "He has two arms to hold the calabash, and six arms to climb, but the calabash is in his way. He keeps sliding down, can't climb the tree."

Alice and Katherine laugh at silly Anansi.

"The little son of Anansi followed him and he watched. Little son said, 'Father, why you not tie the calabash behind you? Then you can climb with all eight legs.'"

Angela pretends to tie the pot on her back. "Anansi thought little son has a good idea. He tied the calabash behind, and up the tree he went." She puts one finger to her head. "But at the top of the tree, he thought, 'Anansi has all the wisdom of Sun God, but little son, he is smarter than me!' Anansi was so angry, he threw the calabash to the ground."

Alice sucks in her breath. "Did it break?" she asks.

Angela nods. "The calabash broke to pieces, and all the wisdom came out. Just then, a big storm came. Rain washed the wisdom into the river!"

Alice groans. "Oh no," she says.

"Wisdom flowed down the river to the sea." Angela shows the flowing wisdom with her slender fingers. "It went all over the world. A little bit came to every person." She touches each of us on our foreheads, first Alice, then Katherine, then me. "Inside everybody, you have a piece of wisdom."

Alice asks, "Am I the smartest in the world like Anansi, now?"

Angela squeezes her hand. "Yes. You are smart enough you don't play with snakes."

Alice shakes her head. "No more snakes."

Katherine snuggles into my shoulder and closes her eyes. Angela's story has made her ready for a nap.

Angela stands. "I will go before my mistress wonders why I take so long."

Mum thanks her for coming and tells her to thank Mrs. Pierce for the baked apples as well.

That night, Alice sleeps fitfully in our bed with me. I try to help her feel better by keeping a cool rag on her forehead. She mumbles in her sleep about snakes and spiders. Finally, when it is almost morning, she falls into a deeper sleep, and I do, too.

The next day Reverend Buck looks in on us. He puts his hand on Alice's forehead and prays for her swift healing. He looks grave and concerned, as if he doesn't really believe that Alice will survive.

Alice eats more of the baked apples, and Mum cooks the egg for her. I still have to carry her to the chamber pot, because the leg hurts too much for her to stand on it. But she doesn't cry anymore, and she plays with Katherine sitting on our bed.

The second night Alice sleeps better, and when I wake before dawn, I see that she is already up, taking her own self to the chamber pot. As she climbs back into our bed, I whisper, "Better?"

"It hurts just a little," she says. "Tell about Anansi?"

I look over at Mum and Katherine, still asleep in their bed. I'm glad Mum is getting some rest. So, very softly, I tell a story, remembering one of Angela's tales as best I can—the one about why Anansi has eight thin legs. When Alice falls back to sleep, I find myself the only one awake.

In the quiet, the feeling of dread starts up again, stronger than ever. It pounds in my head with the rhythm of my heartbeats. It is clear now: poison is coming to the colony.

I remember what I saw when I lifted the veil briefly to feel what Chief Opechancanough thinks of us. I remember the roiling cloud of rage, the fear that we will cause the destruction of his kingdom, his determination to protect his people, his desire to have us *gone*. What better way than to poison us all?

So many ships, I think. There are so many ships arriving, so many new settlers every year, so much Indian land being taken over with trees cut down, houses built, and tobacco planted.

I am sure of what I must do. Poison is coming to the colony and I am the only one who knows. I must be the one to stop it before it kills us all.

Twenty-Eight

BY DAWN I have made my decision. I am going to Elizabeth City. Samuel has always been my help, my partner in following the knowing, and I need him now. I can't go telling Reverend Buck or Governor Yeardley about the message from my mysterious second sight. And I certainly can't get my mother involved in this. Samuel is the only one I can tell. Everyone knows he speaks Algonquian, and so he can easily tell the governor that he heard from the natives about something suspicious going on. He will be able to get out the warning, that no one should eat or drink anything from the natives, without any accusations of witchcraft.

I tell Mum simply what she needs to know. "We will eat only our own food, nothing from the natives," I say to her.

I think of the poisonous plants that grow in the Virginia forest and along the shorelines: jimsonweed, pokeweed, water hemlock. Chief Opechancanough could easily mix poison into bread, or boil the roots in stew, or crush the flowers and berries into wine. Then he could send his messengers to offer this food for trade. Mum readily agrees to no trading. But when I tell her that I must leave for Elizabeth City with the next boat going that way, she is not happy.

She shakes her head. "I will not let you travel such a distance alone," she says.

I want to say I would not be alone. I would be with one of the small groups of settlers who travel between James Town and the other settlements, in shallops or canoes, picking up supplies or delivering goods that they have produced. But I know what she means. I would not be with anyone I know.

I wish I could tell her, "If I don't go, the colonists will be poisoned!" But I don't want to involve her in what the knowing has told me.

I keep my ears and eyes open as I move about the fort, to the well, to pick up rations, to visit Bermuda. The very next morning I hear what I have been waiting for: three Irishmen are heading back downriver. They came from the Dale's Gift settlement to deliver salt that they produced, and to pick up rations.

"Mum, please ask them if I can go," I beg. "They'll be traveling right by Elizabeth City on their way back to Dale's Gift. They are in a shallop so there is plenty of room for me. We could tell them I need to go because Da needs my help." This is the truth. Without my help, Da and Samuel could fall prey to the poison.

Mum shakes her head. "You don't know these Irishmen and they don't know you. They might even be convicts of some sort. You would not be safe."

"But, Mum—" I begin.

"No," she says. "You may not go."

Anger and frustration rise in me. I remember what Samuel said about channeling my anger. I don't want to argue with my mother. I wish I could obey her, but the knowing is prodding me, leading me. I calm myself inside.

"I'll go dig for mussels," I say.

Mum looks at me. She knows full well that once I am out of the cottage, I will be free to go. *Mum, you said yourself that you can no longer protect me*, I think. *Please, stay here and take care of the little ones and let me do what I have to do.*

She seems to hear my unspoken words. She goes to the hearth and breaks a large chunk off the loaf of corn bread that is to be our noon meal. She wraps it in a cloth. Her lips quiver as she hands it to me. "God go with you," she says.

I wrap my warm shawl around my shoulders and run down the well-worn path to the river. If I hurry, I hope to find the Irishmen before they leave. As I near the river, I hear men speaking Gaelic. It is them, the three men, loading supplies onto a shallop.

My heart pounds. Mum is right: I don't know any of

them. All three are short, with black hair and dark eyes. One has a scar along the side of his face. From a knife fight? Another has a flattened, crooked nose. From a fistfight? I have heard that the Irish are prone to drinking too much ale and to bouts of temper. But I must get to Samuel. I suck in my breath and take the last few steps to the shore.

"I need to go to Elizabeth City," I say loudly. "I heard you are going that way."

One of the men, the one with the flattened nose, stands up straight and looks at me. The other two continue putting crates onto the shallop as though they have not even understood my words.

"Ye coming with us, lassie?" he asks.

"Yes," I say as bravely as I can.

He nods and speaks to the other two in Gaelic, motioning as though he is telling them to move the crates to make room for me. The third man, the one who bears no scars from previous fights, looks me up and down. I notice that only one of his eyes moves, and the other wanders off to the side.

I am trembling as I wade into the cold water, and step into the shallop. I have decided to travel with three men who might have chosen to come to Virginia rather than be hanged for various crimes.

Twenty-Nine

—

THE MEN HAVE not asked my name, and so I do not ask theirs. Instead, I name them myself: Flat Nose, Scar, and One Eye. Flat Nose is the only one who has spoken to me, so I assume the other two don't speak English. All he says is for me to stay out of the way and not tip the boat.

I sit up straight on the bench and feel the breeze on my face. The day is mild, and the river is moving swiftly. I comfort myself with the thought that the trip to Elizabeth City should not take long. Da says it only takes half a day if the river helps you along.

Scar and One Eye row with long oars, and Flat Nose steers with the tiller. Scar starts singing a joyful tune in Gaelic, and the other two join in. Even without instruments, it reminds me of the music we have heard in the fort when Irish settlers arrive.

I remember the last time I traveled down this river, with Samuel to go find Angela, and the time before that when Samuel took me to Point Comfort as a baby. This journey has always brought me good things, and I hope that today will be no different.

• • •

As the sun sinks low, I search the shoreline for a break in the trees that will show us where the Elizabeth City settlement is. There might be boats moored at the river's edge, and maybe even a house or barn visible through the bare trees. With the waning sunlight comes a chill. I pull my shawl more tightly around me. My stomach grumbles and I eat the last few bites of my corn bread. Surely we will see the settlement soon, and I will join Samuel and Da for supper.

Flat Nose barks out an order in Gaelic and turns the tiller. But he turns the shallop the wrong way.

"No," I say quickly. "Elizabeth City is on the left, not the right." Don't these Irish know anything?

"The current is pushing us to the right and it's time for supper," says Flat Nose.

"Please, just take me to the north shore and I will walk the rest of the way," I say.

"Can't do that, lassie," Flat Nose says. "We're headed to the south shore to make camp."

"But that's not where I'm going!" I cry.

"Oh yes, it is," he says.

The trees of the river's south shore loom tall where a spit of land reaches out. The men row hard, and we meet the spit of land before the current can wash us past it.

I clench my teeth. This is not what I asked for. I try to calm my fear. *All right*, I think. *They will make camp for the night. Tomorrow we will continue down the river, and arrive early at Elizabeth City. I will only have to last with these men one night and one morning, and then I will be free of them.*

Flat Nose tells me to gather wood for a fire, and the three of them set to work. Scar pulls blankets, a cook pot, and a sack of barley out of the shallop while One Eye cuts saplings and spruce boughs to make a shelter. Flat Nose takes a spear to the river to get fish. Soon there is a pot of barley bubbling and fish roasting over the fire and a shelter built near the fire's warmth. The men sit on logs around the fire, drinking ale and playing a gambling game with a deck of cards.

I take a long drink of river water and find a private place behind a tree to relieve myself. The roasting fish smells wonderful and the three men are having a raucous time at their card game. I look at the fading light in the sky and see the first star peek out. Maybe this one night in the forest with the Irishmen won't be so bad, I tell myself.

The fish is delicious, though I notice that they give me only a small portion while they divide the bigger

POISON *in the* COLONY

hunks of meat. Still, they give me a whole bowl of barley, for which I am thankful. The card game goes on, with them betting coins and knives, a bracelet made of copper, and even a belt buckle. Every time the fire burns low, Flat Nose barks out, "More wood, lassie." I traipse into the forest to find more sticks and logs and return to the fire. I get sleepy and so I sit, hug my knees, and doze off.

I hear the name they've been calling me, "lassie," and snap awake. I start to get up to fetch more wood but see that the fire is burning brightly. The men are gesturing, arguing, and my name is uttered a few more times. I tense inside. What could possibly concern me?

Flat Nose throws down his cards. "Ah, take her," he says angrily. He sees that I am awake. "You belong to him now, lassie," he says, pointing to Scar. "He won you fair and square."

"*Won* me?" I ask, still groggy.

"Ya. He called me bluff."

"He won me from *you*?" I wonder for a moment if I might still be asleep, having a terrible dream.

Flat Nose scoffs at me, as though I shouldn't sound so surprised. "You didn't think your passage was free, did you? You'll have to work to pay it off. Not seven years like the passage from England, mind you. Just a few months."

A few months? Working as an indentured servant? At a strange settlement? My heart races. In a few months we could all be dead from the Indians' poison.

Scar motions to me and speaks to me in Gaelic. Flat Nose translates. "He says bring him his blanket and take his shoes," Flat Nose says. He rolls his eyes. "He's going to have you serve him like he's the blooming king."

I am fuming, but I fetch the blanket and carry it to Scar. He holds up one foot, expecting me to take his shoes off for him. I glare at him and keep my hands at my sides.

"Go on, do what he says, lassie," Flat Nose says. "He's had more than his share of ale tonight."

I open and close my fists. The scar on the side of his face seems to move in the firelight. He speaks to me again in Gaelic, a one-word demand. I scowl. I pull his stinky old shoe off his foot and throw it at him. He has to duck so it doesn't hit him in the head, but he grins and lifts his other foot. Quickly, I pull his other shoe off and drop it.

Flat Nose shakes his head. "Thinks he's the blooming king."

The men wrap themselves in blankets and settle down for the night. "You keep the fire burning, lassie," Flat Nose says. "You can sleep in the boat tomorrow—I'll give you me blanket then."

I look around and see that there are no more blankets. *Of course*, I think, *I am an indentured servant now. I am expected to sit up and stoke the fire all night while they sleep.*

I huddle close to the flames and warm my hands. I

am across the wide, cold river from anyone I know. Tomorrow these men will take me right past Elizabeth City, out into the Chesapeake Bay and around the horn up to Dale's Gift. They will hold me captive there. No one in my family will even know where I am. Now I wish I'd listened to Mum.

Sitting, curled up, I am reminded of the night I spent locked in the storehouse cellar awaiting my trial. As on that night, I think of Angela. When she arrived here, she was across the wide, cold ocean from anyone she knew. *Go inside, Virginia. Find who you are.*

The Irishmen are snoring. The forest is dark and threatening around me. I begin to whisper softly. "I am Virginia. I love the forest and the trees and the life I feel in them that is like the life in me." I blink as smoke wafts into my eyes and burns them. "I am Virginia. I love who I am. And I am *angry!*"

My anger flares. How dare they decide to keep me captive as a servant? How dare they stop me from my mission? In that flash of fury, I want to strike out, to hurt them. But then I calm. I take a breath. These men are commoners, probably even servants themselves. The thought of having their own indentured servant for a little while must be fascinating. And they did give me passage, and food. I continue my whispering. "My anger helps me protect those I love. I can channel it and do the right thing."

The fire is burning lower now. I gather more logs and sticks and build the fire up until it is blazing. It casts dancing orange light on the trees. It is like my fire-breathing dragon but channeled so that it sheds warmth and light but no fighting. I look at the three sleeping men. "Thank you for bringing me this far and sharing your food with me," I say softly. Then I walk off into the dark forest and keep going.

Thirty

———

THE MOON AND stars light my way. I am careful not to stub my bare toes. I will walk until daybreak to stay warm. I will keep the river always on my left and will not get lost. When dawn comes, I will retreat to a hiding place and watch for the shallop to come by. When I know the Irishmen have gone on their way, I will walk back to that spit of land jutting out into the river, where they camped. The shelter is there, and surely there will be burning coals left in the fire. I will be able to get it blazing again. In that spot, the river is narrow, only about three miles across.

From our many hungry winters, I know which roots and plants are edible, so I will be able to easily stay and wait until the next boat comes by. I will shout and signal until the travelers hear me. And whichever way they are going, my only request will be passage across to the other side so that I can walk to Elizabeth City.

As I make my way through the dark forest, I try to feel the life in the trees the way I used to when I was small. I hear a loud creak, and it startles me. But it is only the trees swaying in the wind, their branches scraping together. A hoot owl sends out his echoing call. I know there are things in the forest that can kill me: bears, copperheads, unfriendly Indians. If I were to die out here, without a burial, there would be nothing left but my bones to bleach in the sun.

I keep walking, willing my mind to focus on each step instead of the dangers in the forest. I climb over fallen logs and scratch my legs on brambles. I step on sharp rocks and have to keep from crying out.

When finally I see pink spread across the eastern sky, I am exhausted, scratched and bruised, and very ready to stop walking. I find a place just close enough to shore that I'll be able to watch the river, and just far enough away that I can hide myself behind the trees and brush and not be seen. I don't believe these men have time to spend searching for me. I'm sure they have their own "betters" who are waiting for the supplies and would be angry if they were late.

I sit and lean against a tree, determined to stay awake until I see the shallop pass by. But as I sit, weariness overcomes me and I lay my head back against the tree. *I'll just close my eyes for a moment*, I think.

First, I dream that I am being poked. Then, I realize I *am* being poked. Barely awake, I try to scramble to my feet, to flee. A strong hand grabs my shoulder and pushes me down. I hold one arm above my head, ready to be struck.

When no blow comes, I peek out from behind my elbow. I expect to see the dark eyes and scarred face of my new "master." Instead, I am looking into two pairs of dark eyes.

One is a boy, about my age. He is bare-chested, wearing several shell necklaces and two feathers in the long side of his hair. The other is a little girl. She also wears several shell necklaces and a buckskin skirt. Her hair is cropped short in the front and hangs long in the back. She peers at me with curious eyes.

My mind is racing. Women and girls are protected in Powhatan society. I am unarmed. I pray they will not think I have come to do harm.

A word floats to me, one of the Algonquian words Samuel taught me. "*Netoppew,*" I say. *Friend.*

The little girl bursts into a smile. "*Netoppew!*" she says happily. But then she looks serious as she touches my shawl, my bonnet, the buttons on my dress, fascinated by these new things.

Her brother pulls her hand away and speaks sternly to her in Algonquian. She keeps her hands at her sides, but again she says, "*Netoppew*." We are friends. We mean no harm.

The sun is high in the sky, so I know the Irishmen must have passed long ago. It is safe for me to make my way back to the campsite. I try to stand, but the boy pushes me down again. He *is* armed. He has a bow across one shoulder and a quiver full of arrows on his back. A small club, what the natives call a tomahawk, and a stone knife hang from his apron. These things are for hunting and cleaning game. But they can easily be used against me.

He speaks loudly to me, as though I will be able to understand if he just talks loud enough. I listen closely for anything I might understand. I hear the word *werowance*, or chief, and he says "*Peyaquaugh*," to come with him.

Does he want to take me to his chief and let him decide what to do with me? He motions to me and says, "*Peyaquaugh*," again, and so I rise to my feet and follow these two children where they lead. I imagine running away, but just as quickly I imagine feeling the sharp pain of an arrow piercing my back.

•   •   •

Smoke from cook fires wafts to us. The little girl points ahead of us. "Nansemond," she says. We must be approaching one of the Nansemond villages. I have heard that they are one of our trading partners.

Soon, through the trees, I see the same kind of cottages I remember from my visit to Pocahontas's village when I was small. They are similar in size to our cottages, but with walls and curved roofs made of woven reeds. I smell the delicious aromas of meat and fish grilling over the fires. It makes my mouth water. But then I remember I should not eat anything offered by the natives, lest I become the first victim of their poison.

Once we are in the village, the girl takes my hand and leads me to a big cook pot. It is made of copper, not clay, and I realize it must have been traded from our colony. The girl motions to me to eat, but I shake my head. She looks at me quizzically. She can't figure out why someone who was found starving in the forest would not want food. So, she demonstrates what I am to do. She reaches into a basket for a loaf of bread and rips off two pieces. She hands one to me. She takes the other piece and uses it to scoop up stew from the large pot. It is a thick mix of hominy and oysters. She blows on it to cool it down, then pops it into her mouth, nodding to me. Unless they have poison that kills only English and not little girls, I am safe. I dip my bread into the stew and eat. It is delicious.

A woman comes to turn over the strips of meat being smoked on wooden racks over the fire. This meat will not be for eating today but stored for later in the winter. The woman looks at me curiously, and I look at her. She is bare-chested, with only a leather skirt that reaches from her waist to her knees. Her black hair hangs in a long braid down her back. She wears several shell necklaces and has tattoos on her face and arms. One of the tattoos is of a snake slithering up her arm. I think it makes her look strong.

The boy motions for his little sister to come with him and I am left in the company only of women. An older woman grasps my arm and pulls me over to a large mortar and pestle with corn in it. It looks very much like the ones we use. She pantomimes the motion of pounding the corn to grind it. So here, too, the women must work every waking moment. I am being treated not as a guest, but rather as just another female worker. I pick up the pestle and pound the corn as I have done since I was four years old. The rhythm is wonderfully familiar, and it helps me think.

I will find where they keep their canoes. I will escape at night, when all are asleep. Then I will paddle across the river myself and walk to Elizabeth City. As I pound and think and plan, I hear the boy's voice behind me. "*Peyaquaugh*," he says. Has he brought the chief to decide my fate?

But when I turn, what I see shocks me to my core. She wears the deerskin skirt that all the other women wear, and a deerskin mantle. Her neck is adorned with necklaces made of shells. Her arms are tattooed with images of flowers and birds. Her hair hangs in a long braid down her back, like the other women.

But this woman is different. Very different. Her hair is curly and reddish blond, her skin is freckled, and her eyes are green.

She looks at me and says, "Hello."

Thirty-One

I KNOW THAT some of the native tribes have women as their chiefs. But this woman is not even native, and her clothing is nothing like the beautiful feather mantles the chiefs wear.

"They told me you need an interpreter," she says. She has the same accent as those poor London street children they've been sending.

"Yes, thank you," I say.

She continues, "They think you escaped from a cruel master like I—" She stops herself.

Suddenly I understand who she might be. I have heard of girls and women who disappear rather than be beaten by a cruel master, and who find safety with the natives. "Did you escape from the colony?" I blurt out.

She eyes me suspiciously. "Are you staying with us or going back?" she demands.

"I'm going back," I say.

"Then I didn't escape; I was captured," she says,

defiantly. She adds quickly, "But don't be sending anyone to rescue me. My husband will kill them if they come."

I shake my head. "I promise I will not tell anyone about you." I know that men who have tried to escape the colony and find a better life with the Indians have been brought back to James Town and executed. I certainly would not endanger this young woman.

The boy, who has been patiently listening to our foreign conversation, now speaks to her.

"He wants to know why you were alone in the forest, far from the English," the girl says.

My story is so long and complicated, I decide to tell only the part that is important now. "I am trying to get to Elizabeth City," I say. "To my da."

She interprets, but they both look puzzled. "Elizabeth City?" she asks. "Where is that?"

"Across the river," I say. "All I need is for someone to take me across."

Again, she interprets, and again the boy looks puzzled. Elizabeth City is new, just being settled, so he may never have heard of it. "It is near the old Indian village of Kecoughtan," I say.

They both light up. "Kecoughtan," the boy says, and he rattles off a long sentence.

"He says you will stay here tonight and tomorrow he will take you across the river to Kecoughtan. You will stay in my home."

"Thank you," I say. I am very relieved and grateful. "Thank you so much."

. . .

Her name is Sarah. She takes me to her cottage. An older native woman is sitting on a mat in front of the cottage, holding a baby in her lap. The child has curly black hair and green eyes.

"This is my mother-in-law and my little girl," Sarah says proudly.

The woman and I nod to each other. She bites off a chunk of dried meat, chews it, then spits it out and puts the chewed-up wad into the baby's mouth. The baby girl gums the meat and drools.

"My husband is away on a hunt," Sarah explains as she takes me through the doorway into her home.

Inside the hut there are platforms against the walls with deerskins on them. These must be their beds, I think. There are also shelves above these platforms, where baskets and bowls are kept. In the center of the floor is a fire, and when I look up, I see that a hole in the roof is pulling the smoke up and out. The cottage is cozy and warm, and sunlight streams in through the doorway.

Sarah sits down on a mat in the ray of sunlight and invites me to sit with her. She pulls out her sewing. Her needle is made of bone and her thread is of sinew. She is working, sewing little shells onto a pair of moccasins. She tells me her story as she works.

"Life in London was hard, and even though we were forced onto that ship, some of us thought it might be better here." She scoffs. "Maybe for some it was. Not for me. He about wore out his stick on my back, my master did.

"One day two native men came in a canoe to trade. One of the men was looking at me, and I was looking at him." She widens her eyes to show how they were flirting. "So, I slipped off and laid down in their canoe. When the men found me, they didn't say a word, just paddled out into the river and brought me home." She smiles, remembering.

"We were married as soon as we could build our house," she says. Then quietly, she adds, "He never beats me."

• • •

After dark, I bed down on one of the platforms, under a deerskin blanket, with the fire crackling. Sarah's daughter is tucked in with her, and her mother-in-law sleeps on one of the other platforms. When I was alone in the forest, I imagined many ways I could get myself to Elizabeth City, but none of them involved being this warm and well fed.

In the morning, we go to the communal cook pot again to eat. The stew has had some red berries and pieces of rabbit added. It is still delicious. I am amazed that here, even in winter, they have no rationing. Anyone can eat whenever they want to. Samuel says they have great trust in their gods, Ahone, Okeus, and the Great Spirit that breathes life into all things. They trust that there will be enough, and so no one needs to hoard. In the hungry month of March, if their stores run low, they are all hungry together.

The boy comes to fetch me. He taps his chest. "Pepiscunimah," he says.

"He is saying his name is Pepiscunimah," Sarah tells me. "But we all call him Pipsco."

He nods. "Pipsco."

I tap my chest. "Virginia," I say.

He and Sarah have a short conversation, and she translates for me. "I told him you'll be looking for a break in the trees, that's where the English are," she says.

"*Peyaquaugh*," says Pipsco, knowing I understand this word.

I move to follow him, but Sarah puts her hand on my arm. "Here," she says. "These are for you." She holds out the pair of moccasins she had been working on, beautifully adorned with the small shells.

I catch my breath. "They are beautiful," I say. "But . . . I have nothing to give you."

She holds one finger to her lips. She is asking for my silence in return for this gift, something I would have given her anyway. I put my own finger to my lips. "Until my death," I say.

Sarah nods. "Godspeed," she says.

I follow Pipsco to the river's edge, where several canoes are lying onshore. Together we carry one of the boats to the water, along with two paddles. I don't want to get my new moccasins wet, so I put them in my apron before I wade into the river. I take off my shawl and put it into the boat. I want my arms free for paddling.

Pipsco sits at the back of the canoe so that he can steer us. We take strong strokes as we enter the current, pointed downstream but always moving ourselves closer to the opposite shore.

We watch the north shoreline as it glides past us. Suddenly I see it: a break in the trees and an English barn up on the hill. I laugh out loud, elated. I have finally made it to Elizabeth City!

We guide the boat to shore. I thank Pipsco in English, and he says something back to me in Algonquian that I assume must be "you're welcome." I wave at him as he pushes the canoe back into the river to go home.

As I walk up the hill toward the settlement, my elation dims. I must now face my father, who will surely be furious at me for the way I chose to travel.

Thirty-Two

"YOU DID *WHAT*?!" Da is almost as angry as when he heard I was going to be on trial for witchcraft.

"But it turned out all right, Da," I say, trying to calm him. "I'm not hurt, nothing bad happened, and Samuel can take me home tomorrow so Mum won't have to worry about me."

Da shakes his head and rubs his temples. I have told him only that I have come because I missed him so much, which is part of the truth, so he thinks I endangered myself for no good reason. If I could tell him the whole story, he would not think I was so irresponsible. Samuel, on the other hand, keeps giving me puzzled looks. He knows something more is going on.

Once Da calms down, he and Samuel proudly show me the progress they have made: land cleared for planting, trees felled and being split into clapboard for building, the beginnings of a house, a chosen site for a barn. They have also built a small windowless shed for them to sleep in now, and to be used for storage in the future. Though it is built of wood, it has a roof made of woven reeds, and a hole in the roof to let smoke out. It also has platform beds along the walls, just like the native cottages. I realize that these are things Samuel learned to make when he lived in the Warraskoyack village.

"Let me show her where my house will be someday," Samuel says. "Then we'll get back to work."

I am relieved. He knows I need to talk to him in private.

Da agrees and says he will put some peas on to soak for our supper. It's very strange for me to think of Da cooking. "*I'll* cook supper tonight," I say.

I follow Samuel up the hill to where stakes have been driven into the ground, marking the four corners of his future house. But he doesn't start in about how someday he will live there with Angela and have a family. He simply says, "What is going on, Virginia?"

I tell him all of it, about Alice's snakebite and knowing that we must not eat or drink anything from the natives, and about needing to get the warning out to the rest of the colony very soon.

"I know the Nansemonds are not planning anything," I say. "I could tell from being in their village, they have no anger toward us. Do you think it could be Chief Opechancanough?"

Samuel nods. "Word has come to us that Chief Opechancanough and his brother Opitchapam have changed their names. Opechancanough is now known as Mangopeesomon and Opitchapam is now Sasawpen. This is what chiefs do when they will soon lead a great military strike."

"It sounds like they are planning to get rid of us," I say.

"Chief Opechancanough is ruler over all of the tribes, the way Chief Powhatan was," Samuel says. "He will demand that all the tribes work together to attack us. It won't matter that the Nansemonds consider us their friends. They will have to obey their paramount chief, or face a tortured death."

I shudder. "Chief Opechancanough believes the only way to protect his people is for us to be gone. He is afraid of the prophecy, that we will cause the end of his kingdom."

"Yes," says Samuel. "I think he believes that if he can kill a large number of us, then the rest of us will go back to England and he will be free of us. That is what almost happened after the Starving Time."

"So, our leaders know that the chiefs have changed their names. What will they do to protect us now?" I ask.

Samuel groans. "Nothing!" he says. "I seem to be the only one who really understands what this name change means. I've tried to talk to Captain Newce and Captain Tucker, our leaders here in Elizabeth City. But they think I am worrying for no reason." He puts one hand on my shoulder. "When I take you back tomorrow, I will go right to the governor. You can come with me if you like. We will tell him that Chief Opechancanough is planning to poison the colony."

"He will ask us how we know," I say, "and you can tell him—" To my horror, I suddenly realize that my plan for Samuel to get out the warning is deeply flawed: it would require him to lie. Surely the knowing, if it is from God, would not require either of us to lie. "How will we tell him we found out?" I ask in a small voice.

"You can tell him you learned it from the Nansemonds while you were staying there," he suggests.

"Which is a lie," I say. "And anyway, how could I have heard it from them? I don't speak Algonquian."

"Right," he says. Then he gives me a sideways look. "How did you tell them to bring you here?"

I feel my face flush. I will keep Sarah's secret, but I don't want to lie to Samuel. "Hand motions can say a lot," I say.

He doesn't press me further. "Then I will have to say I heard it from one of the native tribes." He hesitates. "The only problem is that we have had no contact with them for months now. Captain Newce knows that. I could be accused of lying to the governor."

"Treason," I say.

"Well, better for me to be hanged for treason than the whole colony perish," he says.

"And if either of us lies, it will endanger our souls for eternity," I say firmly. "I would rather be hanged as an honest girl and go to heaven. I will tell Governor Yeardley that it is through the second sight that I know this."

Samuel rubs his forehead. "Let me think on it," he says. "There might be a safe, and honest, way to get this done."

• • •

Da starts a fire in the outdoor pit, which they use for cooking when there is no rain. I hang the pot of peas over the fire to get it boiling. Samuel opens their storage barrel and I find some turnips and carrots to add.

"We have only two spoons," Da says.

But I see oyster shells in their trash heap. I pull one out and show him. "Now we have three spoons," I say.

I hear the crunching of footsteps, and when I look up, I see two figures coming toward us across the cleared field. One is an Englishman wearing the simple breeches and jacket of a commoner. The other is a young native man, bare-chested, wearing a breechcloth and leggings.

"Samuel Collier," the Englishman calls out as they come closer.

"I am here," Samuel calls back.

"This man desires an interpreter."

"*Wingapo*," Samuel says. The native man speaks, and Samuel interprets.

"He says that the chief of the Accomack tribe, Chief Debedeavon, will be coming from across the Chesapeake Bay for a visit to our leaders tomorrow. He wants an interpreter present because he has many questions." Samuel speaks to the native man in Algonquian, then says to us, "I have assured him I will be there."

After the two men leave, Da asks Samuel, "What do you think this is all about?"

Samuel glances at me, then quickly looks away. "I guess I'll find out tomorrow."

• • •

I awaken early in the shed. Samuel is asleep, sitting on the earthen floor, leaned up against the wall, since he gave up his bed and blanket for me. Da is snoring on the other platform bed. The fire in the middle of the floor, which we used for heat last night, has gone out. Dim morning light filters in through the hole in the roof.

I push open the shed door and slip behind a tree to relieve myself. It is cold. Winter weather has returned.

I hear a big yawn and Da stumbles out of the shed.

"Good morning," I say.

"G'morning," he mumbles.

I go to the outdoor firepit and get the fire going again. Then I retrieve the cook pot from the shed and uncover the leftover peas. Even with the lid on tight, quite a few ants have found their way into our peas. I scrape out as many as I can and put the pot on the fire to heat. I slip my new moccasins on. They are even warmer than wrapping my feet in rags.

Da joins me at the fire and warms his hands. "I suppose that mild weather couldn't last forever," he says.

I hold my hands close to the fire as well. "So, I guess Samuel and I will go back to James Town tomorrow, then," I say. I want badly to hear what the Accomack chief has to say.

"Absolutely not," Da says. "I will not have your mother worrying another day. I will take you back today myself."

My face falls. Then, in the next instant, I correct my expression. "Wonderful!" I say. "Mum and the girls will be so happy. And I will be happy to have you at home as well."

"I thought you would be," Da says.

Suddenly a terrible thought strikes me. We will be taking their one canoe. Samuel will be stranded in Elizabeth City. He will not be able to come to James Town to warn Governor Yeardley of the threat of poison. Yet I can't tell my father any of this. "I'll go wake Samuel," I say.

When I go back into the shed, I see that Samuel has crawled into the bed I vacated.

"Samuel, wake up. I have to talk to you," I say, jostling him.

He groans. "Leave me alone. I'm finally getting to sleep comfortably."

"But Da wants to take me home in the canoe," I say quietly, urgently. "How will you get to James Town to talk to the governor? You promised you would find an honest way to warn him."

Samuel pulls the blanket up over his head, shutting me out.

"Samuel, we have to talk!" I say, a little too loudly.

Da peeks his head in the door. "Leave him be, Virginia. Let him sleep before he has to be interpreter. He gave you his bed, after all."

And so, I am silent. I will not get to hear what the Accomack chief has to say. We will be leaving Samuel with no boat to get to James Town. I came all the way to Elizabeth City and now Samuel will not be able to help me warn the colony, even if he can figure out a safe way to do it.

But I will do one thing properly today: I will obey my father and go home to my mother so that both of my parents can stop worrying about me. And if, in order to save my family and the colony, I have to confess to Governor Yeardley that I have the second sight, then I will do that properly as well.

Thirty-Three

MUM IS NOT surprised to hear that I traveled with the very men she told me not to travel with. She says I am becoming a difficult child to raise. I apologize to her as best I can. At least she realizes it is the knowing that is behind all of this, and not just me being a disobedient daughter. Above all, she is relieved that I am home safe.

I am thankful to be back home, to wash the clothes I lived in day and night, and to be with my whole family again. Mum and the girls are very glad I've brought Da back for a visit. Alice proudly shows him the fading purple on her leg where the snake bit her.

"You're a brave girl, Alice," Da says.

"I *know*," says Alice.

Katherine shows Da her leg, too, even though there isn't anything to see.

My mind will not let me be. It goes in circles, waging a heated argument between me and me.

Samuel can't get here. You need to just go to Governor Yeardley yourself.

I would never be able to explain how I know these things without confessing to the second sight. Then I will be hanged as a witch.

So? Give your life to save the colony.

If I could be sure it would be that simple, I would do it. But what if Governor Yeardley doesn't believe me? Then my life will be wasted and the colony will perish as well.

You have to take that risk. If you do nothing, then death for the colony is certain.

Or what if he believes me but the accusations of witch-craft spread to Mum? Then my little sisters would lose their mother. I can't let that happen.

So, you're just going to sit here doing nothing while the natives stir their pots of poison, ready to bring it to the colony mixed into bread and stew and—

Be quiet! You are no help at all.

Well, what are you going to do?

This argument has no ending point, and no good answers. All I know is that I must be who I am, nothing more and nothing less. I'm not a gentleman who can speak with authority, nor a leader who can make decisions. I am only a girl whom God has chosen to know something the gentlemen and leaders do not know. If God leads me to speak the warning myself, and lay down my life for the colony, I will do it. But in the meantime, with no natives coming to the fort with food for us, I will wait and hope for a better way.

The next day is Sunday. When church services are over, Bermuda's father gives us the news: Bermuda has finally been accepted as an apprentice at the tar pits. After our midday meal, Mum gives me permission to go visit Bermuda and his family.

I walk through swirling wind to the Easons' cottage. The sky is steel gray with low clouds and I can smell snow in the air. Mrs. Eason welcomes me into their warm cottage.

Bermuda is very excited about his new job. "Now, when they start up the glass house again, I can switch to being an apprentice there," he tells me.

"Well, you badgered those Polish workers until they let you become an apprentice, so maybe you can find someone to badger until they start up the glass house again," I say.

Mrs. Eason offers me a cup of hot tea, which makes me feel very grown-up. Mr. Eason is cleaning his musket and smoking his pipe, filling the small cottage with to-bacco smoke. I blink in the haze and think maybe I agree with King James about the evils of tobacco.

I like Mr. Eason very much. He has already claimed his land at Martin's Hundred, just a few miles down the river from James Town. He travels there to work on his house and land, but since it is so close, he returns home often.

"Have I ever told you about the night we saw St. Elmo's fire?" Mr. Eason asks me between puffs on his pipe.

He has, and it is a wondrous story. "I would love to hear it," I say.

Bermuda settles in at the table with me to listen, and Mrs. Eason puts us to work shelling corn off dry cobs.

"I've never seen such a storm," Mr. Eason begins. "For four days and nights, the ship tossed like a wild horse, wind a-howling, rain coming sideways so hard, I could scarcely open my eyes. We dropped the sails just before the waves got so big, they'd have capsized us for sure."

Behind his story is the crackle of the fire, the *toc-toc-toc* of our corn kernels dropping into the bowl as we break them off the cobs with our thumbs, the creaking of the cottage in the February wind. But in my imagination, I am on a ship in the tropics in a roiling storm at sea.

"With the sails down, the wind caught the rigging and set up a high wailing, like a thousand ghosts lost in purgatory."

I shudder. Bermuda looks at me and gives a devilish grin. He has heard this story a hundred times and enjoys seeing other victims scared by it.

"I thought for sure we would die!" Mr. Eason's voice rises. "We all thought we would die, drowned and lost forever, our bodies torn apart and eaten by sharks."

I stop shelling and hold my breath, anticipating the next part.

"That's when we saw it." Mr. Eason's voice goes low and mysterious. "It started as a soft glow, up atop the mast. I thought maybe I was already dead, seeing the light of my Lord. But no, the others around me saw it, too, and there were shouts and gasps, even some cursing from the rougher sort.

"The glow grew brighter and bigger, floating there atop the mast, until men dropped to their knees and begged God for forgiveness for whatever evil they'd done in their lives."

I close my eyes, to better see that glow in my imagination. A ball of fire, holding out hope of safety and salvation.

"It hung there, like it would set fire to the rigging, though it never did, and the storm raged on."

Bermuda pipes up. "That's when you made God a promise about me, right, Da?"

"That's right," Mr. Eason says. "I promised God that if I could live long enough to see my child born, I would make sure to tell this story and scare all his friends."

I snicker, and Bermuda rolls his eyes. Mrs. Eason says, "Edward, that is not what you promised."

"That's true," Mr. Eason says. "I promised that I would make sure he got to go fishing every Sunday."

"Da!" Bermuda objects. "Tell the real promise."

Mr. Eason takes a puff on his pipe and blows a smoke ring into the air. "I promised God that if I could live to see my child born, I would love and protect him my whole life."

Bermuda grins. It's his favorite part of the story.

"But the storm only got worse!" Mr. Eason continues. "The sea washed over the deck and gushed into the hull, full of holes as it was by then. Every man and woman, sailor and passenger alike, worked to pump and bail and plug the holes with whatever we could, even meat from the larder. We threw our trunks and barrels overboard, hoping to lighten the ship. Then just before dawn on the fourth day, I saw the twinkling of a star. I felt the wind blow a little less hard. I sensed that the rolling of the ship had settled down. And when I heard the shout, 'Land ho!' I knew we were saved."

"Tell how I got my name," Bermuda says.

"Well, of course, because the land we sighted was the island of Bermuda, and that's where you were born," Mr. Eason says.

"Tell about the play and that Mr. Shakespeare," Mrs. Eason urges him.

I've heard it before, but I certainly don't mind hearing it again, how the writer William Shakespeare heard of the storm and shipwreck of the *Sea Venture*, and wrote a play about it. He called it *The Tempest*, and it was performed in the theater in London.

"Those actors who play it onstage should have been in

the real tempest!" Mr. Eason says. "They know nothing of what it was truly like."

There is a knock at the door, and when Mrs. Eason opens it, snow swirls into the cottage. It is Choupouke, carrying a basket.

"Come in out of the snow," Mrs. Eason says cheerily.

I stare at Choupouke's basket. My stomach tenses. Choupouke's family members, who still live in the Indian village, often give him things they have made, like clay pots or bowls, or food when they know we need it. Since Choupouke speaks our language, he is chosen to do the trading. He trades for what we have, like cotton clothing or metal tools. I hold my breath, waiting to see what he has in the basket.

The adults make polite small talk. Then Choupouke lifts a piece of deerskin off his basket and asks, "Dried venison. You want?"

"No!" I shout it.

Everyone looks at me.

"I—uh," I stammer, not knowing what to say. "I just think we have plenty of food, right, Mrs. Eason?"

But Mrs. Eason has her fists on her hips. "Well, Virginia, I know there are some who think they are so high and mighty they won't eat what the natives bring, but that is not us."

"I didn't—" I begin, but I have no way to defend

myself. My family would never refuse food from the natives—until now.

Suddenly I know what I have to do. I need to touch Choupouke to see if he has any malice in him. Surely if the meat were poisoned, he would have been warned not to eat any of it. I step over near him, as though I need a better look at the meat. Carefully, I brush his hand. I feel calmness, eagerness, interest, but no malice. I am relieved.

In the next moment, Choupouke surprises me. He lightly brushes *my* hand. I feel something new this time, something I can't quite grasp. It's a little like admiration, but not quite. Then I look up at him and see it in his eyes. It's *attraction*. He thinks I'm pretty!

I feel my face flush bright red and I scurry back to my chair. I sit very still, looking straight ahead.

"Do you approve, Virginia?" Mrs. Eason asks me teasingly. "Are we allowed to trade for some meat?"

I give a quick nod, keeping my eyes on the far wall.

"What's wrong with her?" Bermuda asks.

"Nothing is wrong with me," I snap.

Mr. and Mrs. Eason discuss the trade with Choupouke. Would he like a pair of woolen socks Mrs. Eason just knitted? Choupouke points to his bare feet and shakes his head. They settle on a piece of flattened iron, excellent for making into a tool, for the whole basket of meat.

After Choupouke leaves, Bermuda and I finish shelling the pile of corn while discussing how best to catch crayfish for fishing bait. At least he doesn't think I'm pretty.

"Virginia, isn't it time for you to be helping your mother?" Mrs. Eason asks after a while.

I agree. I wrap my shawl around my shoulders and step out into the swirling snow. As I walk home, I think of how, if I could touch each person who offers us food, I would find the poison. I could keep us safe if I were allowed to do that. But it would be impossible to tell this to anyone and keep *me* safe. And there are too many plantations and towns now. I can't be at all of them. For a moment, I stop walking and close my eyes tightly. I don't want the arguments in my head to start up again.

"I will give my life if that is what You ask," I whisper. Then I open my eyes and walk through the falling snow back to our cottage.

Thirty-Four

BY MONDAY MORNING, Da is feeling torn about leaving us. Between Alice's snakebite and my near indentured servitude, he is afraid we might not be safe on our own.

"But I can't expect Samuel to work by himself," Da says. So, reluctantly, he packs up the cabbages Mum has given him from our root cellar, and we all follow him down to where the canoe has been pulled up on the riverbank. He gives us hugs and kisses.

Alice is unhappy and whiny. "I don't want you to go," she says, tears welling up in her eyes. "Why do you have to go when Samuel is coming here?"

Da ignores her question and pats her on the head. Mum gives me a panicked glance. I scoop Alice up into my arms. "Let's go see if we can find a frog," I say. "Do you think frogs like snow?"

When I have her out of earshot, I whisper, "Is Samuel coming today?"

"Yes," Alice says. She sniffles.

I glance up. Mum is helping Da carry the boat down to the water, but she is watching us. I nod to her. It is all I can do. Yes, Samuel is coming today. If she can think of a way to stall, to get Da to stay here, we'll have another day with him rather than sending him back to Elizabeth City to work all by himself and wonder where Samuel is. I know that as reluctant as Da is to leave, it shouldn't take much to get him to stay.

I hear Mum yelp and see her fall to her knees.

"Alice," I whisper. "Do you still feel like crying because Da is leaving?"

"Yes," she says.

"Then do it—cry. *Loud*. Right now," I tell her.

I lead a wailing Alice back to where Mum is on her knees on the ground. Da is bending over her. Mrs. Hudson, who has come to the river to fetch wash water, rushes over to help. Katherine begins to cry now as well.

Over all the noise, I hear Mum reassuring Da. "I'm all right, John. I just got dizzy for a moment."

Da tries to help Mum up, but Mrs. Hudson stops him. "No, sir, if she's dizzy, the last thing you want is her standing up." To Mum, she says, "You just sit there, Ann, until you feel better." Then she snaps at me, "Can't you get those children to quiet down?"

I try to calm the girls. "Mum is going to be all right," I say.

But Alice doesn't even want to hear about Mum. "I don't want Da to leave!" she cries.

Mrs. Hudson narrows her eyes at Da. "Leave? Where are you rushing off to? You can't leave your wife in this state."

Da shakes his head. "No, you're right. I can't. I will stay."

Alice stops her wailing in an instant. "You were right, Ginny, it worked. And now Da will get to see S—"

"Alice!" I say quickly. "Leave Da alone so he can help Mum." I pick up Katherine and take Alice's hand. "I'll bring the girls back to the cottage so they'll be out of the way," I say. *And explain to Alice that she has to keep Samuel's arrival a secret*, I think.

• • •

Once Mum is settled in bed, and both girls are playing with their dolls on the floor, Da goes out to fetch wood for the fire.

"Did you really get dizzy?" I ask quietly.

"The thought of your da not being here and all this going on with Samuel and that chief and you worried about food from the natives—that makes me plenty dizzy," she says.

"Mrs. Hudson showed up just in time, too," I say.

"She was an angel, saying all the right things," Mum says. "And Alice was a help, making it sound like the world would end if Da didn't stay."

"I know," I say. "I told her to."

Mum raises her eyebrows at me just as Da comes back through the door, his arms loaded with wood.

"There's something going on," Da says. He drops the wood onto the floor and picks up the poker for the fire. "The leaders from Elizabeth City, Captain Newce and Captain Tucker, have just arrived along with Chief Debedeavon of the Accomack tribe, and Samuel. Everyone is long-faced. I don't know how serious it is, but I'd say it's a very good thing I didn't leave you girls here alone."

"Yes, John," Mum says. "A very good thing."

"May I go see, Da?" I ask urgently.

Da says yes and I rush out the door.

People are gathering to watch the four men walk through the fort. The chief is tall with broad shoulders, wearing a magnificent mantle woven of shimmering blue feathers. Captain Newce, Captain Tucker, and Samuel look small and plain by comparison.

Samuel sees me and breaks from the group to come over to me. He leans in close. "You did it," he whispers. "The warning is almost complete." Then he straightens back up and marches ahead.

"What is going on?" a gentleman calls out to the men.

"We have come to see the governor," says Captain Newce. "After we have met with him, an announcement will be made and you will all be informed."

There is murmuring among the colonists, speculation as to what is going on.

"Is that chief a prisoner?"

"Of course not. He was not shackled."

"They could have informed us now instead of making us wait."

"Why is Samuel Collier involved in this? He's a commoner."

"He's an interpreter. Lived with the natives when he was young."

I watch as the men arrive at Governor Yeardley's house and go inside. *You did it. The warning is almost complete.* I am safe. Samuel is safe. And the colony is safe.

. . .

I have to wait until evening to have a moment alone with Samuel. Mum does not object to me going with him—she trusts whatever is going on.

We leave the fort and head to the near woods. There, we stop and listen for a moment to be sure there is no one else around. Then Samuel launches in.

"When Chief Debedeavon arrived with his guards, I met with him and Captain Newce and Captain Tucker. He asked lots of questions, about how many settlements we have and what land we are using up and down the river. I interpreted his questions, and their answers. The chief seemed nervous, like he had something on his mind.

The English call him 'The Laughing King,' but he was not in a laughing mood at all. At one point, everyone was silent. I knew that no one but he and his guards would understand my words in Algonquian, so I asked, 'What about the poison?'"

My eyes grow wide.

"You should have seen his face!" Samuel says. "Out came the whole story, how Chief Opechancanough wanted his tribe to gather as much water hemlock as they could find, because it grows in great abundance where they live. He said he did not want to do it, did not want to poison us. He also said he doesn't think we are using too much land."

"And you translated it all?" I ask.

"Of course," he says.

"And then you brought the news to Governor Yeardley?"

"Yes. The governor is leaving today to go visit every one of the cities and boroughs to get the warning out. The word is spreading through James Town now: we are not to eat or drink anything that comes from the natives. And soon the word will reach Chief Opechancanough that his plan has been revealed."

"Thank you, Samuel," I say. "Thank you for listening to me and believing me."

"Of course I believed you, Ginny," he says. "I always have."

As we walk back toward the fort, Charles comes striding down to meet us. "I have important information for you," he says, with an air of supreme authority, looking only at Samuel. "While you were out picking weeds or whatever it is you do in the woods, an announcement was made." He clears his throat, as though he is about to introduce the king. "We are not to eat or drink anything the natives offer us—not that I would do that anyway, but people like you might."

Just for fun, I ask innocently, "Really? Why not?"

Charles grunts with annoyance. "I'm not telling *you*; you're just an ignorant girl. I'm telling Samuel."

Samuel crosses his arms over his chest. "Well then, do tell me why not."

Charles leans in conspiratorially and speaks in a low voice. "They were going to poison us. They had a plan." He straightens up. "But their plan has been foiled, thanks to the good gentlemen and leaders of our colony."

I clench my teeth together. Not a word must escape my lips.

"Yes, the good gentlemen, of which you are one, Charles," Samuel says. "Thank you very much for informing us. If not for you, we may have perished. Now if you don't mind, we really must get back to picking weeds."

Charles turns and marches ahead of us back to the fort. I am about to explode. Once Charles is within the gates, I can finally blurt out, "Why didn't you tell him that you were the one who translated the meeting with our gentleman leaders?"

"He'll find out soon enough that I was translator. It's no secret," Samuel says. "And then he'll be good and embarrassed that he acted like a know-it-all."

When we get back to James Town, everyone is discussing the plot to poison us.

"They were going to kill us *all*!"

"They hate us."

"Not all of them. The chief of the Accomacks saved us."

"I'm never eating their bread again. It's hard and heavy as a rock anyway."

I say goodbye to Samuel as he heads off to see Angela, and I make my way back home. I feel buoyant. So much darkness and heaviness has lifted. I have done what the knowing asked of me and my part in all of it will remain a protected secret. Now I can go back to my normal life and stop being a "difficult child to raise."

An orange cat trots over to me and rubs against my leg. I lean down to scratch her under the chin. "This is a good day," I tell her. She closes her eyes and purrs.

Near our cottage, I walk by two men talking. I hear only one sentence, one snatch of their conversation:

"How will they try to kill us next?"

Thirty-Five

DA AND SAMUEL go back to work on our homestead in Elizabeth City for several more weeks, but in mid-March we are happy to welcome them home for tobacco planting. The birds return, too, and it is time to plant peas and onions in our garden plot.

By April, the ships begin to arrive. Most of the new colonists are the usual crop of servants: convicts from the prisons, drunks picked up off the streets of London and Bristol, homeless children, and poor farmers who were kicked off their rented land by wealthy landowners. Sadly, there are also more kidnapped children, lured with candy and forced onto the ships.

All these new servants are sent to work the tobacco plantations so that the gentlemen who run the plantations can make more money. And while the gentlemen grow rich, their servants die from lack of food and from having to live in the woods because there are not enough tents and cottages for everyone.

A new sort of trade has begun: the buying and selling of men and boys. The gentlemen argue and barter, wanting the strongest and fittest servants for their plantations. Some servants are lost and won in card games, the way the Irishmen did with me. Da says if they would just feed their servants well and give them a dry, warm place to sleep, then they wouldn't always need to buy new ones. He overheard two gentlemen complaining that out of every hundred servants that get sent to their plantations, seventy-five of them die within the year.

Some of the new colonists are called Puritans. Mum says they wanted to purify the Church of England, but the church didn't like their ideas and so they have come here where they can be free to have their religious beliefs. They are sent down the river to live at the Lawnes Creek settlement.

Later in the spring, Chief Opechancanough himself comes to meet with Governor Yeardley. He says he never had any plans to poison us, but that Chief Debedeavon lied in order to end our friendly relations. He says his greatest desire is to have peace between us and for his people to be our friends and helpers. Governor Yeardley, and most of the colonists, want to believe that this is true. Many of the colonists go back to trading with the natives for food, and no one drops dead of poison. I know that it is Chief Opechancanough who is lying. And I am greatly relieved that it was Chief Debedeavon, and not me or Samuel, who told Governor Yeardley about the plot to poison us.

George Thorpe is still trying to convince Chief Opechancanough to send the native children to his new school. By early summer, Mr. Thorpe comes up with a new way to try to bribe the chief: he decides to build him an English-style house. Da and Samuel are called away from the tobacco fields to help build the house, since they are excellent carpenters. Mr. Thorpe wants the house to be fancy, not just a cottage.

◆ ◆ ◆

In midsummer, when Da and Samuel have been gone for weeks helping to build the chief's house, Alice wakes up one day and begins to sing a happy song about Da coming home. She is like a little harbinger, always letting us know the day Da will be returning. This knowledge of when people she loves will arrive is the only way the knowing has manifested in her, and so Mum is not too worried about her.

"Is your da coming home today?" Mum asks her.

"He is," Alice says.

"Shhh. Don't tell anyone," Mum says, making it sound like a fun game. "It will be our secret, all right?"

Alice whispers, "I'll keep the secret." Then she goes back to singing her song, but more quietly.

Da is home in time for supper. "Lucky again," he says. "I always seem to come back on stew days."

Mum gives Alice a furtive glance and quickly taps her finger to her lips. Alice's eyes are bright with the secret. "We've had only loblolly *forever*," she says.

I quickly change the subject. "So, has Chief Opechancanough seen his house yet?" I ask. "Does he like it?"

Da digs into his bowl of stew and talks with his mouth full. "He is fascinated with it," he says. "We put a lock with a key on the front door. He's never seen anything like it. He locks and unlocks that door at least a hundred times a day."

"Well, that should convince him to send all the native children to live at Mr. Thorpe's school," Mum says sarcastically.

"I know, it's ridiculous," Da says. "But what can we do? The Virginia Company officials know almost nothing of life here, and yet they come up with plans and send people to carry them out. All we can do is follow orders."

"I don't like it when their plans put us in danger by angering the natives," Mum says.

"Neither do I," Da says. "Their plans are so often like poison to our relationship with the natives."

Poison. It is more deadly than the poison of my spider bite or of my sister's snakebite. It is even more deadly than the water hemlock Chief Opechancanough wanted to use against us. The poison is now seeping out, little by little, each time George Thorpe tells the natives that our ways are better than their ways and they must send their children to his school to be reeducated. It spreads out each time the Virginia Company officials sit in London and make decrees that more native lands now belong to colonists. It leaks into our lives every time trees are cut down on a swath of land to build English houses and plant tobacco.

I remember what I overheard that night, months ago: *How will they try to kill us next?*

Thirty-Six

WHEN I SEE the tall, dark figure with white wings and feathers enter the fort, I am not afraid. I run to get Samuel at the soldiers' barracks to tell him that Nemattanew will need an interpreter. I find Samuel with a group of young men.

"Ah, Jack of the Feather is back," says one of the men, and he claps Samuel on the back. "Maybe he wants you to help him stick more feathers to his chest."

The other men laugh, and Samuel glares at them, stone-faced. As we walk away, I look back. They are cackling and strutting around pretending to be roosters. "Why didn't you make them stop?" I ask. "Nemattanew deserves more respect than that."

Samuel stops walking and turns to me. "Those boys are as ignorant as rocks in the river. They don't know anything about respect. I won't even bow to their level by correcting them."

I blink at him. "I never thought of it like that," I say.

He continues walking. "You should," he says. "Nemat-tanew is a great warrior. He knows it, and all of his men know it. He has their respect. He has been in many battles and never been wounded. His men believe he is immortal."

I remember when I first saw Nemattanew and how I thought he was a magical creature. I wonder if he might be magical after all.

When we get to the center of the fort, we find Nemat-tanew in conversation with a gentleman, Mr. Morgan. Actually, they are trying to have a conversation with their hands and a few words, and it looks as if they are not get-ting very far. Nemattanew sees Samuel, calls out, *"Pey-aquaugh,"* and motions him over. What follows is a long sentence in Algonquian, with Samuel's translation: Would Mr. Morgan be pleased to accompany Nemattanew on a trading mission to the Pamunkey tribe?

"Yes, certainly," says Mr. Morgan. "I will have my ser-vants prepare my things for the journey."

A couple of days later, Nemattanew returns. His canoe is already laden with furs, baskets, and clay pots for the trading mission. Mr. Morgan's servants carry his goods for trade down to the canoe: a brass kettle, pewter spoons, cotton cloth, scissors, an ax, a hoe, and flat pieces of cop-per. Some of it has been given to him by families who hope he'll be able to trade it for food to supplement their rations. My mother, of course, has given nothing to the trading mission. We will eat from our own garden and our rations no matter how vehemently Chief Opechancanough denies that he ever wanted to poison us.

• • •

In September, it always seems that the crickets get louder, chirping all day and night. The sun slants low and hot, and the smell of ripe tobacco is everywhere. Da and Samuel work all day in the tobacco fields along with the other laborers, but in the evenings they talk and plan. They will soon be back on our own land, this time hopefully never to return to laboring for the colony.

"We will move in late December," Da tells us. "As soon as this tobacco harvest is over, I'll go get our house ready for the winter and cut enough firewood. That way, we'll be able to prepare our seedbeds for tobacco during the winter and be ready for March planting."

Da says he will also make trips back and forth, carting our furniture and stores of food, and then, finally, Mum and the girls and me. Whenever I think of that final day of moving, it stops my breath. We'll be leaving everyone, Bermuda, Angela, Jane. At least I'll finally be done with Charles.

One of the first ships to arrive in September brings us fascinating news: we are no longer the only English colony here in the New World. Last December, a ship called the *Mayflower*, carrying a group of settlers, landed many miles north of here. They have named their colony Plymouth. The settlers have built their houses and storehouses and have made peace with the natives who surround them, the Pokanoket tribe of the Wampanoag people.

I listen to the stories with eagerness. I will never see any of these new settlers, as they are much too far away. But I love knowing they are here on this land, and that they are living in peace with the Pokanokets. If they can live in peace, I hope that it is possible for us to continue to live in peace as well. Our days are intertwined with our native neighbors. Some of them live and work among us in James Town, and the other settlements as well. Many come each day from their villages to help the settlers in the fields or to build houses or fell trees. They have breakfast with English families and then go to work together. In return for their time, we pay them with the things we have that they value: cotton cloth, metal tools, copper and beads, scissors and knives. We are living at peace and benefitting from what we share with each other.

There are changes coming to James Town: Governor Yeardley's term is nearly over. As each ship arrives, I wonder if our new governor will be on it. I hope that the Virginia Company is sending us a good leader.

In October, ships come one after another, nine in all. Da says we now have over twelve hundred colonists living in our settlements up and down the river. There is one ship that, when it lands at James Town dock, causes great excitement. When I hear the shouts of "Ship ashore!" I tell Mum I will go fetch water so that I can see what is going on at the docks.

This ship brings the news we have been waiting for.

"Yes, he is the new governor."

"A nobleman of fine stature."

"And married to the niece of George Sandys, who is to be our new treasurer."

"Good. The Virginia Company has chosen well."

The name of our new governor is Sir Francis Wyatt. He is dressed in the finery of a nobleman, but he doesn't carry himself in that haughty way that Governor Dale used to. Yet for me, Sir Wyatt's arrival is not the main interest of the day.

There is a small group of new colonists: men with their wives and children, all gesturing and talking loudly in another language. They are short people, with dark hair and round eyes. Their language is definitely not Gaelic, so I know they are not Irish. Who are they?

I listen to the conversations around me, trying to find a hint as to who these foreign people are. When I hear it, when I learn who they are and why they have been sent here, I take off running. I run away from the docks, across the stubbled tobacco fields, to where smoke is rising from the tar pits.

"Bermuda!" I shout. I am so loud, all the men working in the tar pits stop and look at me.

"Bermuda, it's your wife come to call you to supper," one of the men says, and they all laugh.

But the teasing doesn't even bother me. I shout my news at the top of my lungs. "They've sent workers from Italy, Bermuda. *Glassworkers.* They're going to start up the glass house again!"

Thirty-Seven

BERMUDA WASTES NO time getting himself onto the work crew that is rebuilding the glass house. I see him one evening on his way home from work. He is dirty, exhausted, and very happy.

"How is the work going?" I ask.

"We're repairing the walls and rebuilding the furnaces," he says. "Next we'll put on a new roof."

I've never seen him so alive and excited. I suddenly feel bad for all the times I discouraged him about his glassmaking dream. What I have learned about myself has helped me see him more clearly. "I'm so glad for you," I say. "And . . . I understand now. I didn't understand before." I search for the right words. "Glassmaking is your dream. You have to do it because it's who you are, and you have to be who you are."

He tilts his head and looks at me, as though I have put words to something he has felt but not been able to express. "Yes," he says. "That's exactly how it is."

"Well, thank goodness they sent those Italians," I say.

He beams at me. "I'd better get home before I fall over," he says. "I've been skipping the noon meal." He hurries toward his cottage.

As I watch him go, I wonder why in the world he wouldn't be eating his noon meal.

The next day I stop by the Easons' cottage. Mrs. Eason is stirring a pot of barley and fish stew, so it's not that the Easons have run out of food.

I don't even have to ask Mrs. Eason about Bermuda's strange new eating habits because she immediately starts in about it. "Virginia, would you please take some stew to Bermuda? He won't come home. All he wants to do is work, work, work. I send him with some bread, but that's not enough."

We wrap a bowl in rags so it won't burn my hands. I put a spoon in my apron pocket and walk carefully down the well-worn path to the glass house.

The glass house is noisy with hammering and clanging. I find Bermuda straining under the weight of an armload of large stones. He lets them drop in front of one of the furnaces. Two of the stones break. I am not prepared for what happens next.

One of the Italian men marches over, swings his arm wide, and smacks Bermuda in the side of the head. Bermuda staggers. A familiar rage rises up in me. In a few steps, I am in front of the man, ready to tell him to leave my friend alone. But one glance into his eyes stops me. There is something wild about him. He is wiry and strong. I know instantly that he would kill me if he were angry enough.

I bring the bowl of stew to Bermuda. "Are you ready to go back to the tar pits yet?" I ask.

"No," he says. He rubs the side of his face, which is very red, and already beginning to swell. "But I'm ready for them to send Vincenzo back to Italy."

I look over at the man who slapped him. He is furious, arguing with one of the other Italians, waving his arms and gesturing at the broken stones.

"All you did was break some rocks," I say. "It's not like there aren't plenty more."

"He's always mad," Bermuda says. "Leone, the one he's yelling at now, speaks some English. He told me that Vincenzo hates it here. He complains that all we have is corn and hardly any wheat. They call our corn porridge 'polenta' and Vincenzo doesn't like it. He wants something called 'pasta.' I don't know what 'pasta' is, but it is made from wheat."

Bermuda gratefully takes the spoon and bowl from me and sits down on a wooden plank to eat. I sit next to him. In between bites, he continues to talk. "Leone also said that in Italy, every town has its own dialect of Italian and there is no one else from Vincenzo's town here, so it's hard for him to talk to anyone except his wife."

"At least he can talk to her," I say.

"Yes, but she is afraid of him," Bermuda says.

I look at Bermuda's swollen face. I hope Vincenzo doesn't do the same thing to his wife. "Does it hurt?" I ask.

He shrugs. "It's not bad."

It is almost noon, and in small groups, the men leave to go home to eat. Finally, it is quiet in the glass house, with only me and Bermuda.

"What do you do when they all leave? Why won't you go home, too?" I ask.

"I stay here and work in peace without being afraid that Vincenzo will hit me," he says.

Bermuda has waited so long for his dream to come true, and now he has to work with this wild man. I wish that somehow I could fix it for him.

"Are they going to send him back to Italy?" I ask hopefully.

"No, I just wish they would," he says.

Bermuda finishes his stew and hops up. "Let me show you what we're doing."

First, he gestures over our heads, where the frame of a roof is already up. "We're finishing the new roof soon," he says.

Then he points to a medium-sized furnace built of rocks and mortar. "This is the fritting furnace. You mix together river sand, crushed oyster shells for lime, and ashes for potash, and put it in here to start to heat up."

He takes me to look at the biggest furnace, which is

broken and crumbling. "We have a lot of repair work to do on this one," he says. "It's the main furnace and it gets the hottest. It gets so hot, it makes the sand, shells, and potash mixture into melted glass." He picks up a long metal rod. "You put the end of this rod into the oven to pick up a lump of molten glass. Then you shape it"—he twirls the rod—"you blow air into it to make it hollow"—he blows through the rod. "Then you use this wooden paddle to flatten the bottom before it cools off too much.

"When you've got your drinking glass or pitcher or whatever you've made, you put it in here." He points to the smallest oven. "That's the annealing furnace, where the glass cools down slowly so it won't crack."

Bermuda's eyes shine with enthusiasm. I can see exactly why he puts up with Vincenzo for the chance to be around this thing he has wanted for so long.

"You already know how to make glass, from start to finish," I say.

"Leone says as soon as we've got things up and running, he'll teach me," he says. "It's not as easy as it sounds."

"I'm glad some of the Italians are nice," I say.

"They're all nice except Vincenzo." He looks at me sideways. "Can you give him the summer flux?"

I blush, remembering my threat the last time someone punched Bermuda. I play along. "Hmmm. I'm afraid it's too late for that since it's already autumn. Would you settle for a different illness? Scurvy, maybe?"

"Anything that would send him to bed and keep him away from here is fine with me," Bermuda says.

I know Bermuda considers this "witch" talk only a joke.

"I'd better go," I say. "If I don't get home soon, I'll miss my own noon meal."

"Thanks for bringing the stew," Bermuda says.

◆ ◆ ◆

Mrs. Eason begins to depend on me to bring food to Bermuda, and my mother doesn't mind, so I get to see the glass house taking shape. One day I get there and Bermuda is up on the framed roof, helping to fasten down woven reed mats to close the roof in. The next day he is slapping handfuls of wet clay between the large stones of the biggest furnace.

"That's the one that will get the hottest, right?" I ask. "Where it all melts, and you put the rod in to pull some out to make a drinking glass?"

"Yes," he says. "And the repairs are almost done." He brushes a shock of hair out of his eyes, smearing a streak of clay onto his face.

"Stay still," I say. I take a lump of wet clay and draw lines on his face, the way the natives do when they have a dance or a feast. "There," I say, "now you're ready for a celebration."

Bermuda takes my cue. He stretches out his arms and begins to dance in the rhythmic, flat-footed way we've seen the natives do. The Italians and the other workers are quitting work for the midday break, and they stop to watch Bermuda. Someone begins to drum a stick against a flat board. Others begin to clap in time or tap stones together. There are two native men on the work crew and they drum in rhythm with their hands on wooden planks.

As I watch Bermuda, it is as though I can feel his heart flying: his dream is taking shape. Soon he will be a glass-maker.

One by one the musicians quit to go home to eat, and Bermuda ends his dance. Sweat rolls down his face, smearing the clay lines.

"We're almost ready," he says. "As soon as the clay on this furnace dries, we'll start the fires. It will take a few weeks to get hot enough to melt the glass."

"Weeks?" I ask, amazed.

He guides me behind the glass house, where large piles of wood are stacked. "Workers have been cutting hardwood for weeks. But first we need to dry the wood in the furnaces because it is fresh-cut. Then, once it's dry, we have to burn it down to charcoal since charcoal burns hotter than wood. *Then* we can burn the charcoal to melt the glass."

I shake my head. "That's a lot of work. And a lot of waiting," I say.

"I've waited this long," he says. "I can wait a few more weeks."

Thirty-Eight

IT STARTS AS a breeze that lifts my hair and makes me look into the sky at the low dark clouds.

"It's going to rain," I tell Alice. "Rinse what you have soaped up, and let's go." She is learning to wash clothes in the river, and doing quite well at it.

The wind picks up quickly and by the time we carry the wet laundry back to the cottage, it is whipping our skirts against our legs. We rush into the cottage and shut the door behind us. Mum has a pot of melted bayberry wax and she is dipping strings into it to make us a new batch of candles.

"Storm's coming," I say quietly, because Katherine is napping.

Mum nods. "I could smell the rain. Hurry and close the shutters."

I go outside to close and latch the shutters. It has begun to rain and people are scurrying, taking in laundry, ushering small children indoors. I am relieved to know that Da and Samuel are working inside one of the tobacco barns. The crop is now being twisted and rolled and wound into balls to be ready to ship to England.

Back inside the cottage, Alice says, "The wind wants to blow our cottage away."

Mum and I both laugh. "Of course it won't do that," I tell her. "You've seen lots of storms before. It will rain and the wind will blow and there will be thunder and lightning, and then it will be over and the sun will come out."

"There is no thunder," Alice says.

By now our shutters and door are rattling and we can hear sheets of rain hitting the roof. Alice is right. There is no thunder. And the wind is stronger than in any storm I've ever seen.

An eerie, high whine starts up. It is the wind blowing through the holes in our walls, spraying rain with it. The cottage is shaking. Mum and I look at each other. "What is this?" I ask. "It is no normal storm."

The wind howls. Rain hits the cottage like handfuls of rocks. There is a loud crash as something blown outside slams into our cottage. The noise wakes Katherine and she begins to whimper. Alice gets onto the bed with her and hides under the covers. Over the din I hear Alice's voice. "It wants to blow our cottage away!"

Mum has stopped working on her candles.

"What should we do?!" I ask her. Surely she will know how to keep us safe. But she just shakes her head, her eyes wide.

Suddenly a gust of wind blows our door wide open. Rain shoots across the room. I lay my weight against the door and try to push it shut but I am not strong enough. Mum joins me and we both push with all our might. We get it closed and Mum holds it. "The table!" she cries.

I shove the table across the room. We lift it up on end and brace it against the door. The wind is a loud low rumble and a high whine. It is everywhere. Alice and Katherine are both crying, hiding under the blankets.

Mum and I do the only thing we can do. We pick up the two little ones, hold them and tell them everything will be all right, and we pray for God to deliver us from this storm.

◆ ◆ ◆

Those who have been through storms at sea say it was undoubtedly a hurricane. It has uprooted trees and swept away cottages. No one was killed, but many colonists have been injured. The commoners come to us with cuts and bruises and broken bones. Mum and Jane and I treat them with bandages, poultices, and splints. The "better sort," the gentlemen and nobles, go to the doctor to be treated.

◆ ◆ ◆

The roof of the glass house is completely gone. I bring Bermuda his food one day, and see that the inside is flooded, with pools of water to splash through as the workers keep the fires burning in the furnaces.

"We'll nail down boards this time," says Bermuda. "No more thatched roof." He is cheerful. This latest setback can't damage his hopeful mood.

I survey the group of workers. "Where's Vincenzo?" I ask in a low voice.

Bermuda gives a little smile. "Sick," he says.

I raise my eyebrows.

"Good job," he says, then punches me in the arm to let me know he is only kidding.

"I hope he stays sick," I whisper.

• • •

In late November, with the tobacco harvest shipped off and the cottages repaired, Da and Samuel are ready to leave for Elizabeth City. Bermuda's mum and da have already moved to their new house on Martin's Hundred, and so Bermuda now lives in the soldiers' barracks. He has promised his parents he'll come live with them in March to help get ready for planting time on the farm. I know it will be hard for him to leave the glass house, but he is a good son.

James Town is so crowded now, Mum says another

family will be in our house before we're all loaded onto the boat. It feels very strange to be going to a new home and for my home to become someone else's.

Mum worries about Bermuda. She says he is too young to be living on his own and might not be getting his full rations. One day she sends me with porridge and bread for his midday meal. When I get there, Bermuda is alone, tending the fire in the furnace where the wood is being dried and made into charcoal. He opens the small door to add more wood. The heat blasts him, blowing back his hair, and his face turns red. He shuts the furnace door and comes to take the food from me.

"Thank you," he says. "I love your mum's cooking."

I narrow my eyes at him. "It's plain porridge," I say. "It's no different from anyone else's porridge. What do you boys eat in those barracks anyway?"

"Some of the boys know how to make loblolly," he says.

He definitely looks thinner. But it is clear that not even being hungry could turn him away from his dream of making glass.

"How much longer now?" I ask.

His whole face lights up. "Just a few days and Leone says we will mix the sand and crushed shells and potash and start it heating. Then it will take a while to melt."

We hear voices as the workers start arriving after

eating. There is one loud, angry voice above the rest. Vincenzo.

"Sometimes he comes back drunk," Bermuda whispers.

I grimace. If it were one of the regular colonists caught drunk, he would be punished severely. But I've heard that these Italians are above the law because they are the only ones who can do the glassmaking.

"He was so violent toward his wife, the governor was afraid he would kill her," Bermuda says quietly. "So they sent her back to Italy on one of the ships. Now Vincenzo is madder than ever."

Vincenzo's eyes are wild. As he nears us, he glares at Bermuda. I take hold of Bermuda and start to pull him away. Vincenzo picks up a crowbar. He shouts a stream of angry words, walking toward the large furnace.

Everyone is quiet now, watching, ready to protect themselves from this crazy man.

Vincenzo swings the crowbar. With all the force of his rage, he brings it down upon the furnace. There is a loud crack, and smoke billows into the air. Bermuda shouts, "No!" and rushes at Vincenzo. Vincenzo raises the crowbar over Bermuda's head. I scream and dash forward. I crash into Bermuda, knocking him to the ground.

There is loud shouting. "Get him, lads. Tie him up!"

Three men grab Vincenzo. They hold him facedown on the ground. He struggles and yells, but they shove his face into the dirt. Someone tosses them a rope and they bind his ankles and tie his wrists behind him. Then they tie his wrists to his ankles.

"There, now he's tied like the pig that he is," one man says.

Bermuda and I pick ourselves up. "Are you all right?" I ask.

He looks at the furnace, which is spewing smoke and losing precious heat. His face is pained. Does he even realize he was just nearly killed?

"Bermuda, you can fix the furnace," I say.

He nods and wipes his eyes.

"That man almost killed you," I say.

"Maybe we can put river clay over the break," he says. "We'd better do it quickly, before too much heat is lost." He starts toward the door.

I grasp his arm and jerk him toward me. "Are you even paying attention? It's not safe for you to be working around Vincenzo anymore. You need to go back to the tar pits. It's too dangerous here."

He just stares at me as if he doesn't comprehend my words.

"What if next time I'm not here to push you out of the way?" I demand. "What if he kills you?"

Bermuda looks over at Vincenzo where he is struggling against his ropes and cursing in Italian. "I hope that if he does, I get to make some glass first," he says. Then he marches out the door to go get river clay.

I take a few steps to follow him, but then I stop. It dawns on me that Bermuda is living his life the way I am now living mine. He is claiming his truth, and being exactly who he is, no matter what the danger and no matter what the cost.

Thirty-Nine

TOWARD THE END of December, Samuel and my father come from Elizabeth City with two rowboats, ready to take all our household things, and us, to our new home. On moving day, we start before sunup. We dump the corn husks out of our mattresses and fold up the linen, ready to make new mattresses from the husks Da has saved for us in Elizabeth City. After breakfast we load our pots, spoons, knives, plates, drinking flasks, and bowls into a crate and cushion them with our blankets. Alice and Katherine are excited, running back and forth, trying to help but mostly getting in the way.

Angela comes to visit, looking sad. "James Town will not be the same without your family," she says.

I hug her tightly. "You will be with us soon," I whisper in her ear.

Angela helps to carry our things to the boats. Samuel kisses her right there in front of all of us, which makes Alice giggle.

Bermuda comes to say goodbye. He is holding something wrapped in a rag. "I have a present for you," he says. He hands it to me. It is warm. When I unwrap it, I am astonished. It is glass. Green, heavy glass. It looks like it used to be a drinking flask that somehow got squashed into sort of a lump, but it is *glass*.

"It was my first try. I just took it out of the annealing furnace so I could give it to you," he says.

"*You* made this?" I ask, still hardly believing.

"I know it's not very good. Leone says I have a lot to learn. But he says I didn't burn my hand off, so that's a great start."

"It is *amazing*," I say.

"I wanted you to have it before you left," he says.

"But it's your first one. Don't you want to keep it?" I ask.

He shakes his head. "I'll make more." He looks down at the ground. "I'm going to miss you," he mumbles.

I stare at the warm lump of green glass in my hand. It blurs, and suddenly I know there is something I need to say or I will never forgive myself. "You've been a good friend, Bermuda," I blurt out. "I'm going to miss you, too."

"I'll come visit you," he says. "I'll steal a boat if I have to."

"Come on, you two," Da calls. "There's more to load."

Da has decided that we can fit our chairs into the boats, but we will leave our table and our bed frames for the next family. He and Samuel have been using their carpentry skills at the new house and have already built most of what we need.

As Bermuda and I carry chairs from our cottage to the river, he chatters on about the glassmaking. "You get the lump of molten glass on the end of the rod, right?" he says. "Then, the faster you twirl it, the more it spreads out." He puts his chairs down for a moment and makes me stop so he can demonstrate the exact twirling motion. "Then when you blow through the rod to make the piece hollow, you have to blow just right. You should see what those Italians can do," he says. "They are like magicians."

"What about Vincenzo?" I ask. "Is he still hog-tied?"

Bermuda laughs. "He complains that the sand is no good, that he can't make decent glass with this river sand. If you saw what he did make, you wouldn't even believe it. Perfectly shaped pitchers and goblets. He is the best of all of them."

"So that's why they put up with him," I say. "Be careful around Vincenzo, *please*."

"I will," he promises. "At least he's happier now that he is making glass."

When we get to the river, Angela is holding Katherine and she has Alice by the hand, keeping the girls out of the way. Mum and Da are still loading one boat. Samuel is already sitting in the other rowboat, which is fully loaded, his oars ready.

"Katherine, you want to come with me?" Samuel calls out. "I'm good at taking babies down the river without their mothers."

The joke is meant for me and my parents, about the time when I was that baby. But Katherine whines, "No!" and clings tightly to Angela.

"Don't worry, you're going with Mum," Da tells her.

Suddenly, I want to leave. Right now, this minute, get the goodbyes over with, be done with James Town fort and start on this new adventure. "Mum, will you be all right without me if I go with Samuel?" I ask.

She nods, and I splash into the cold water of the river. Samuel steadies the boat so I can climb in. I sit atop a wooden crate and wave to Angela and Bermuda. "Goodbye. Come see us," I call.

Samuel rows out into the current and we drift away from the little group onshore. I feel a tug at my heart. But then I look up into the sky, blue with the morning sun. New. It will all be new.

"We have good luck when you and I go down the river together, right?" I say to Samuel.

"Yes, we do," he says, and pulls strongly on his oars.

Forty

——

OUR HOUSE IS *huge*. Instead of being one room like our cottage, it has three entire rooms: the kitchen and then two separate rooms for sleeping that Da calls bed rooms. It also has a wooden floor instead of plain earth. "There won't be so many spiders," says Mum.

We have not just one but three shuttered windows, one for each room, and the most amazing thing is that in the kitchen, there is a diamond-shaped piece of clear glass set in the wall. Sunlight glints through it, and I realize it will let light in even when it is stormy or cold out because we won't have to shutter it closed.

"What is that?" I ask Da.

"It's a window, only with glass," Da says. "They're used in England all the time. We just don't have very many of them in the colony, but surely you've seen them in church and some of the fancier houses."

I blush. Of course, I've seen them. "I guess I just never thought I'd live in a house that had one," I say.

The whole house smells deliciously of newly cut wood. The hearth is wide and welcoming, and Mum immediately gets a fire going. Then she puts Alice and Katherine to work stuffing dried corn husks into our mattress linens. I set to grinding corn with the mortar and pestle.

By the time evening comes and a light rain has begun to fall, we have newly made mattresses and a big pot of porridge to fill our bellies. Everything seems to be going well until bedtime.

I am washing up the dinner bowls when I hear Alice's angry voice. "No! *I* made it, and it does not belong in here."

I look up to see Alice dragging a mattress out of one of the bed rooms and into the kitchen.

"Alice, this is a bigger house," Mum says patiently. "Don't worry, Virginia and Katherine will be with you."

"No!" Alice stomps her feet. "It is not right."

Da steps in. "You made the mattress, but I built this house." He drags the mattress back into the bed room and puts it on the bed frame.

Alice begins to whimper. Da picks up Katherine. "You want to sleep in your new bed room, don't you, Katherine? Alice, look how good Katherine is being. Come on, let's go see your new room." He carries Katherine into the room, and I assume he puts her down on the bed, because the next thing I hear is loud wailing. "No bed room!" Katherine cries.

"I don't want to sleep in a *bed* room!" Alice whines, and she joins in the wailing.

Samuel arrives back with an armload of firewood. "What happened here—did the king die?" he asks.

Da comes back in carrying a very loud Katherine. He looks at Mum helplessly.

"Maybe just this one night," Mum says. "Today was such a big change."

And so, we make Alice and Katherine happy by moving aside the table and chairs, dragging both mattresses into the kitchen, and all bedding down together, including Samuel, who thought he'd have the kitchen all to himself.

"The floor is made of wood, so it's almost like a bed frame," Mum says before she blows out the candle.

Alice is especially happy because she gets to sleep next to Samuel. "She still wets the bed sometimes," I say in the dark, from the other side of the mattress.

Samuel groans.

"I do not," Alice insists.

"Every once in a while," I say.

"Good *night*," Mum says emphatically, to let us know it is time to stop talking.

"Good night," we all mumble, and we drop off to sleep in our new home.

•   •   •

The next few days turn bitter cold, and no one wants to sleep away from the hearth fire, so each evening we drag the mattresses into the kitchen for our family bed. Da says it's like the inns in England, where there is one big bed and all the travelers who stop in for the night sleep in it whether they know each other or not.

Despite everything Da and Samuel have done, we still have lots of work to do. Mum and I tie up our skirts and get a ground fire going on the land that has already been cleared. We control the fire with metal rakes to keep it creeping along, burning up dry leaves, twigs, roots, and the smaller stumps that have been left behind. The fire clears the debris, preparing the ground so that we can plant, and it also creates potash, which will help our crops to grow.

Da and Samuel take the girls and go to work on finishing the barn. Alice and Katherine think they are helping, fetching tools and pieces of wood, but mostly they are being kept safely away from the ground fire.

On Christmas Day, we attend church in Elizabeth City. It is not a long walk from our house to the church, only a couple of miles. It is strange to go to a new church in a new place with new neighbors and a new minister, Reverend Jonas Stockton.

After services, Mum looks very happy, chatting with the other women. I look to see if there is anyone my age.

But most all of the children are small, like my sisters. Alice and Katherine have already found two little girls to skip around with.

Then I see my mother talking to a girl who looks just a little older than I am. Maybe she is telling her about me? I walk toward them, but when the girl turns, I see that she is pregnant.

"When your time comes, have your husband send for me," Mum says.

I stop and stare. The girl *is* just a little older than I am. The same way Mum was just a couple of years older than I am now when she married Da. I do not want to get married soon, or have babies, or any such thing. I turn and hurry off in the other direction.

Da and Samuel are talking to Captain Newce, the manager of Elizabeth City lands.

"Yes, come spring we'll make sure you get a few chickens from the supply ships," Captain Newce tells my father. "You'll need a good strong barn—we've got plenty of raccoons and foxes like to wipe out a flock in a night. It's not like James Town fort, where the palisades keep most of those critters out."

"Speaking of the palisades," my father begins, then he leans in close and I hear the words "natives" and "threat," and I know he must be discussing whether or not we are safe here with no palisade walls or watchmen to protect us. Captain Newce seems to ease his mind, because Da's next questions are about getting a mule in the springtime to pull a plow so we can plant, and also a cow so we can have milk and cheese. Captain Newce says he'll see what he can do.

As we walk home, Mum clucks her tongue about the fact that there is no midwife in Elizabeth City. "I'll have to help as best I can," she says.

I have a burning question to ask, but I'm not quite sure how to put it. Finally, I blurt it out. "Mum, I don't have to get married at fourteen like you did, do I?"

"Of course not," she says. "You can wait as long as you want to marry. With the way they keep sending more men than women, there is no chance you'll end up an old maid."

Samuel tugs on my hair. "Wait until you're at least fourteen and a half," he says.

I swat at him, but he darts out of the way.

Forty-One

——

EACH DAY I wake in our new home, it feels more familiar. Our days are filled with hard work, our nights spent cozy in bed in front of the hearth. Mum and Da say in the spring we'll start sleeping in the bed rooms.

In James Town, we relied on rations the ships brought and meat shared among the colonists when a cow or goat was butchered or from the gentlemen's hunting. Here, we must make our grain last until our own corn ripens, and we will be able to do our own hunting.

One day, Samuel shows me the bow and arrows he made when he lived in the Warraskoyack village years ago. Kainta, the chief's son, taught him how to make the bow from a sapling and string it with sinew. Then he chipped the arrowheads from stone, chose the straightest wood for the arrow shafts, and tied feathers to the arrows to help them fly true.

"I replaced the sinew on the bow last winter, but the arrows could use some new feathers. Once the arrows are ready, they will shoot more accurately than a musket," Samuel says. "Then I will teach you how to use them."

I try not to look too surprised. Hunting has always been for the men to do, both among the colonists and among the natives. But if Mum will give me time away from my chores to go hunting with Samuel, I will bring back plenty of meat for our brine barrel, and we will eat well all winter.

Samuel and I work together. We use feathers from a turkey Da shot with his musket and tie them to the arrow shafts with sinew. Then Samuel shows me how to rub pokeweed berries on the shafts to bring back the purple color, for decoration.

Samuel and Da have been cutting the long grasses, collecting hay for when we will have our own animals. Samuel takes a big armful of hay and wraps sinew around it to bind it. "See if your mum will give you a piece of rag," Samuel tells me. "Then we will have our target for you to practice on."

Mum does not easily give up a rag. "What if someone gets hurt and I need this for washing and bandaging the wound?" she demands. She is not happy about Samuel teaching me to hunt.

"Just a small piece," I beg. The smaller the piece of cloth, the harder it will be for me to hit the mark, but the better hunter I will become.

She finally gives in, and I bring Samuel a piece of

cloth a little bigger than my hand. First, he takes poke-weed berries and crushes them in the center of the cloth, making a purple blotch. Then he binds the cloth to the hay. "This is your target," he says.

It is a good thing that the bow and arrows are more accurate than a musket, because at first all I can hit is the ground. But every chance I get to leave my work, I practice. I squint at the white cloth with the purple center, willing my arrow to fly directly into it. I hold my arms as still as I can, slow down my breathing, concentrate. Soon, I can hit the bundle of hay with each arrow, even though I have yet to hit the cloth target.

The first time my arrow pierces the cloth, I whoop so loud, Mum comes running to see what has happened. When she sees that I am fine, just practicing my shooting, she walks back to the house, shaking her head.

The first time I hit the purple center, Samuel is watching. I do not whoop and yell; I simply turn to him and grin.

"Time to get some meat for your family," he says.

Samuel tells me of a clearing nearby where he has seen a lone six-point buck. "He comes at dusk to browse," he says.

Once again, I try not to look too surprised. I had assumed my first kill would be a rabbit or a turkey. But if Samuel thinks there is a buck we can kill, I will certainly try.

The very next day, Samuel and I go to the clearing before sunset. I wear my moccasins to keep my feet warm, and to better walk quietly in the forest. Samuel shows me how to test the wind—wet my finger in my mouth and hold it up to feel the slight cold breeze. We find a place to hide in the underbrush, downwind of the clearing. That way, the buck won't be able to smell us when he comes.

Samuel hands me the bow and the quiver of arrows. He is giving me the first shot. "You want to aim just behind where his front leg attaches to the shoulder," he tells me. "And pull your bowstring back smoothly all the way to full draw. You want your arrow to go through the lungs, and hopefully the heart. That will bring him down fast." Samuel has told me about the native way of respecting the beasts, so that in the kill, the hunter tries to cause a quick death with the least possible pain. He has also explained how the natives always give thanks to the animal for giving up its life, and to their god Okeus for providing meat.

We are silent, waiting. There are only a few birdsongs on this cold winter day. I am watching, listening, alert. My mind is clear and calm. Shafts of low sunlight filter through the trees.

Time passes quickly and soon the sunlight dims, then turns to shadow. I hear crackling in the leaves and swing my head to look. Only a bird, hopping, poking around for insects. The light dims further. I hear the crunch crunching of footsteps. They come closer. I catch a glimpse of antlers above the underbrush. I suck in my breath silently. It is him.

Samuel nods to me. Slowly, so the buck will not notice, I rise up on one knee and position my bow.

He is browsing, eating whatever he can find, searching the ground for acorns and nosing the underbrush for berries. Little by little he makes his way toward our hiding place. I imagine the bundle of hay and the white cloth with the purple center. The buck's shoulder, with his lungs and heart just behind it, sits within my mental target. Suddenly, I realize he is close enough. Very slowly, I pull the bowstring back to full draw.

I send up a prayer. I want to kill, for meat for our family, but not cause too much pain to this great beast. My heart is racing. I hold my breath and let the arrow fly.

The arrow strikes. The buck runs. Samuel puts a hand on my arm, his eyes still on the buck's path. "We will wait," he says. "We will let him fall without chasing him."

Samuel takes the bow and quiver from me. After a few moments, he leads me on the buck's path, following the trail of blood.

He did not make it far, but when we find him, he is on the ground, flailing and struggling, his eyes wide, my arrow stuck in his side. Tears spring to my eyes. *I have caused this pain.*

Samuel has already drawn another arrow. At close

range, he drives the arrow deep into the buck's lungs and heart. In seconds, he is still.

I look up at Samuel. "Did I do it . . . wrong?" I ask. "He felt pain."

Samuel puts a hand on my shoulder and gives me a little shake. "You did it *right*," he says. "He has already gone back to the Great Spirit, and it took only minutes." He frowns. "When I was your age, I was on a hunt with Captain Smith. We heard a commotion and here came two wolves chasing a doe. We climbed a tree to be safe and watched. They must have already chased her a long way, because she looked exhausted and terrified.

"Each time she fended off one, the other one jumped at her hindquarters, biting and ripping. Finally, she fell. They continued ripping at her flesh. It was a long time before she lay dead."

I let out a shaky breath.

"You gave that buck a very quick death," Samuel says. He hesitates, and then adds. "We should all be so lucky."

I kneel down and touch the buck's soft ears, then run my hand along the smooth hair on the top of his head. "Thank you for giving your life so that we will eat," I whisper.

Samuel has brought a sharp knife, and he shows me how to carefully cut back the hide on the buck's belly, and then open the belly to remove the entrails. "We'll leave the guts for the wolves," he says.

We cut out the heart, liver, and kidneys, and Samuel puts them in a leather pouch he has brought. "You can make us a proper venison-and-kidney pie," he says.

"I want to make moccasins for my sisters from the hide," I say. I remember watching Sarah as she made the moccasins I am now wearing. "I'll need sinew for my thread. Did you learn how to make a sewing needle from bone slivers?" I ask.

"Yes, I did," he says. "When I lived with the War-raskoyacks, I learned how to use each part of the deer. We will make spoons from the top of the skull—that will make your mum happy."

We each take hold of an antler and drag the buck back home. When Mum sees us, she is thrilled.

We hang the buck in our barn where it will be safe from predators while the meat cools. Samuel teaches me how to remove the hide, using a sharp knife. Then I slice up the heart and liver, and fry them in a skillet over the fire. It makes a delicious supper for our family.

As I watch Alice and Katherine, Mum, Da, and Samuel enjoy the fresh meat, I feel good that I have helped to keep them healthy during this cold, lean winter.

Forty-Two

THE WEATHER TURNS warm for a few days in late January, and Samuel thinks of an excuse to go to James Town.

"I'll see if they have any spare rations for the outlying plantations," he says.

We all know that there will be no extra rations, but we also know that Samuel wants very much to see Angela, and so we encourage him.

"Yes, go see if you can bring back some eggs or fatback," my mother says.

"Tell Bermuda we are doing well," I say. "Tell him I am very happy with the glass piece he made for me." It doesn't really work as a drinking flask, but I keep it on the kitchen windowsill where the sunlight makes it shine.

We pack Samuel up with food for his trip, messages for Bermuda and Jane and Angela, and orders to bring us back all of the news of James Town. Then we send him on his way, paddling up the quiet waters on the edge of the river.

Several days later when Samuel returns from James Town, he is not alone. When I see whom he has brought with him, I feel squirmy inside. It is Choupouke.

"I've brought us some good strong help," Samuel calls as they come walking up the hill from the river.

"*Wingapo*," Choupouke greets us. He glances at me, then looks away. Katherine and Alice come running. They grab Choupouke's fingers and pull him in a circle.

"He'll be closer to his family here and can visit them more often," Samuel says.

"Welcome," Da says. "We can certainly use the help."

My mind is racing. *Will he eat with us every day? Where will he sleep? Not in the kitchen with all of us!*

I have been avoiding Choupouke since last winter at Bermuda's cottage when he touched my hand and I knew what he was feeling for me. He is too shy to pursue me, but I have often caught him looking at me when he thinks I won't notice. It was easy to ignore him in James Town with so many people around. But here it will be just us. I must be scowling, deep in my worried thoughts, because Samuel grabs my arm.

"What are you so peevish about?" he asks quietly.

"Where is he going to *sleep*?" I snap at him in a whisper.

Samuel looks blank for a moment, as if he hadn't

thought of that little detail. Then he waves away my concern. "He can sleep in the barn. He brought his deerskins and furs to keep warm."

That evening at supper, Samuel shares the news he has brought from James Town. Cecily, who is now happily married to William, just had a healthy baby boy. The glass house is turning out glass, and Bermuda is getting better and better at it. Jane and her husband, Robert, send well-wishes. And of course, Angela sends her love to all of us.

I keep my eyes on my food. I decide that if I could ignore Choupouke in James Town, I can ignore him here. All I have to do is stay quiet and polite and not ever look at him.

It's not that he is ugly or ignorant or mean. In fact, he is quite handsome, with smooth copper skin and calm dark eyes. He is kind and soft-spoken, and he loves to make my sisters laugh. I would be happy to be his friend, the way I am Bermuda's friend. It's just that when he touched my hand, I felt something different from friendship— something meant for a girl who is ready for romance and marriage, which I certainly am not.

• • •

My plan of ignoring Choupouke goes on for about a week. Then one day the men are off working, the girls are napping, and Mum and I are kneading dough for bread.

"Why do you dislike Choupouke so?" Mum asks me.

"I don't dislike him," I say quickly. "I just . . . I feel that he likes me too much."

"Yes, I catch him looking at you sometimes," Mum says. "I don't blame him. You are growing into a lovely young woman."

"I'm a *girl!*" I slap the dough down onto the kneading board.

"Yes, you are still a girl. No one is rushing you," Mum says.

"I feel like Choupouke wants to rush me," I say.

Mum shakes her head. "He is only admiring you. He knows full well that we have too many men and not enough women. It makes sense that some of our men marry their women, but you will easily find an English man to marry."

Now I punch the dough harder than it needs to be punched. "I don't want to marry an English man," I say.

Mum raises her eyebrows at me.

"I mean, I know I will marry one—but they are all so . . . *English.* I know what they say about me when they talk, that I am wild, that I grew up here in the wilderness and don't know English manners because you and Da were too busy surviving to teach me. They say the same thing about Bermuda."

Mum raises her eyebrows again and just looks at me.

"What?" I ask.

"Bermuda," she says. "You are both more Virginian than English."

"Right," I say. I knead my ball of dough, and suddenly it dawns on me what Mum is suggesting. "You mean *marry* Bermuda? That's silly, Mum. He's only a boy, and he's my friend."

"Yes, and you are only a girl, but in a few years, you both will have grown up."

I am quiet, thinking. I picture Bermuda with his tight curls and impish face. Will he ever really grow up? "Maybe he won't like me when he becomes a man," I say. "Maybe he'll be sweet on some other girl who hasn't bossed him around his entire life."

Mum lays a damp cloth over the dough to let it rest. "Either way," she says, "I think you can speak to Choupouke now and then without him thinking it means you want to marry him."

• • •

Alice wants to learn words in Algonquian, and so Choupouke has been teaching her. They sit on the floor and I decide to join in. He teaches us to count to ten: *necut, ningh, nuss, yowgh, paranske, comotinch, toppawoss, nusswash, kekatawgh, kaskeke.*

Then he points to Da. "Man," he says. "*Nemarough.*"

And to Mum. "Woman. *Crenepo.*" He holds up Alice's foot and points to her new moccasin. She giggles. *"Moccasin,"* he says. "It means shoe."

Alice tries out a word from their last lesson. "Net-oh-pew," she says, and pats Choupouke's chest.

"Yes," he says. He glances at me, then back to Alice. *"Netoppew.* Friend."

Forty-Three

IN LATE FEBRUARY we have a spell of very cold weather, and Choupouke walks to his village to visit his family and sleep in a warm house for a few days. I am feeling much more comfortable around him, but I still wouldn't want him sleeping with us.

At church, Mum reminds the young pregnant woman to have someone fetch her when her time comes to give birth. From the looks of her, it will be any day.

And so, several days later, when there is loud pounding on our door in the middle of the night, Mum jumps up, knowing it must be time. It is the woman's husband, frantic with fear. Mum hurries off into the night.

When Mum returns in the early morning, she looks exhausted. Everyone is still asleep, but I have been up waiting for her. She slumps down into a chair. I go to the pot of hot chamomile tea I have heating on the fire and ladle it into a cup for her. She takes it gratefully.

"Are they well?" I whisper. I would hate to have her

first delivery as a solo midwife end in tragedy.

She nods.

I look at her quizzically. If all is well, then why does she seem so distraught? I decide to be brazen about using the knowing. I reach out and lay my hand on her arm. What I feel shocks me: terror.

"Mum, why are you so afraid?" I ask, still in a whisper.

She startles, as though she had forgotten that the knowing lives in me strongly now and guides me. There is no use trying to hide her feelings. "I am afraid of what will happen in the next few days," she says. "If the mother becomes ill, or the infant dies . . ." Her voice trails off. I decide, rather than force her to talk about it, I will find out for myself why this scares her so.

I grasp her hand and immediately I see a scene: a kitchen with stone walls; a woman a little older than my mother. The woman has Mum's same black curls, the same round, dark eyes, but it is not Mum. There is a baby playing on the floor, and a little girl stands at the fire.

The scene unfolds in my mind's eye: There is loud pounding, then suddenly two men burst open the door and stomp into the room. All is confusion. There is shouting, the baby screaming, the girl grasping onto the woman as she is dragged off by the two men. I let go of Mum's hand, not wanting to see any more of this horrific memory.

"Your mum," I whisper.

"She delivered babies for the common folk," Mum says. "No one expected all babies to live, or even all mothers to live through childbirth. She did the best she could and she was very good.

"One day, Mum delivered a child for the wife of a merchant, of the yeoman class. He had all the money in the world, and when the child died at three days old, he had all the money he needed to charge my mother with witchcraft and see it through the courts to the end."

I stand up behind her and wrap my arms around her to comfort her. "You would never have left that girl to deliver without help," I say. "Now all you can do is trust God with their lives." I hesitate. For a moment I feel how strange it is to be talking to my mother this way, offering her counsel as if I am the mother and she the daughter. I continue. "And you must trust God with your own life."

She turns to look at me and touches my cheek. "When did you become so wise?" she asks.

Our conversation has begun to wake the sleepers. Katherine yawns loudly and says, "My hungry," at which point everyone else in the bed begins to stir and yawn and sit up. I go to the fire to stoke it and get the porridge heating.

• • •

With Choupouke's help, the men make quick progress. Soon the frame of Samuel's house is up. By early March, Samuel is again longing to see Angela.

"Go on, then," Da says. "You'll just be in the way here, moping around with that long face."

So, we send Samuel off again with messages for friends and orders to collect all the most interesting gossip from James Town. I give Samuel a flat stone I found, an absolutely perfect skipping rock, to give to Bermuda if he hasn't already left for Martin's Hundred to help his parents.

After Samuel leaves, the feeling begins. I should be calm, assured by Captain Newce that we are safe here even without palisades. I should feel comforted to have Da with us, with his musket always ready with powder and shot, and his sword hanging on the wall above the hearth. I should feel relieved to know that the danger of Chief Opechancanough's plan to poison us is past, that he has vowed to keep the peace between our people. I should feel happy and safe with plenty of food still in our storage and spring coming soon. And yet I do not feel calm. I feel a rhythm of warning, like the drums of the natives, or the steps of the African dancers. It says, "Keep watch, keep watch, keep watch."

. . .

When Samuel returns, he brings us greetings from our friends, all except Bermuda, who has already left for Martin's Hundred. He also brings very sad news. Nemattanew is dead. It happened just a few days before Samuel got there.

Nemattanew had gone on another trading mission with Mr. Morgan, and came back several days later wearing Mr. Morgan's cap. There was no one in James Town to translate. All Nemattanew could do was make it understood that Mr. Morgan was dead. With no explanation, it was assumed that Nemattanew had killed him.

"But they were friends," I object. "And Nemattanew is a warrior. He kills in battle. He had no reason to murder a friend."

"Exactly," Samuel says. He clenches his fists. "I wish I had been there to translate for him."

"Or me," Choupouke says. His face is dark with sadness. Nemattanew was a great warrior, a respected hero. It is a huge loss for him.

Samuel continues his story, telling us how a group of men in James Town were convinced that Nemattanew was a murderer and they shot him.

Choupouke shakes his head. "He always tells us the white man's bullets cannot hurt him."

"Yes," Samuel says. "As he was dying, he kept slapping the ground where he lay, saying, 'Bury here, bury here.'

I think he was begging to be buried in James Town so that his people wouldn't know that the white man's bullets killed him."

Choupouke gets up and walks outside into the cold. Through the window I see him go toward the forest, toward the path to his home. Samuel starts to go after him, but Mum stops him.

"Let him go," she says. "It is a shock. He will need time alone and time with his people."

Katherine and Alice have been playing quietly with their dolls, but now they feel the tension in the room. Alice climbs up on Mum's lap, and Katherine climbs up on Da's.

"What of the peace?" Da asks. "Has Chief Opechancanough spoken about this?"

"Messengers were sent to the chief with the news of Nemattanew's death," Samuel says. "Governor Wyatt sent apologies, said it was an accident. Chief Opechancanough sent back the message that this one death, even though it was of a great warrior, will not be the cause of war. He said the sky should sooner fall than that he would break the peace between our people."

Samuel's words should be comforting, but they are followed by heavy silence. I look at Alice and see her scowling. I wonder if the knowing is prodding her.

"I don't like that chief," Alice says.

He wants us gone. I don't dare say it. Chief Opechancanough believes that the only way to protect his people, to keep them safe and keep his kingdom intact, is to get rid of us. And now, by killing Nemattanew, our men have committed an act of war.

As my heart pounds in my ears, it sets up the now-familiar rhythm. "Danger, keep watch, danger, keep watch, danger, keep watch."

Forty-Four

CHOUPOUKE IS GONE for a few days, and when he returns, he seems different, much more serious and moody. I hear him and Samuel talk together in Algonquian and I hope that Samuel is helping him to sort out his sad feelings.

When Choupouke is with Alice and Katherine, playing their games or teaching them Algonquian words, the heaviness seems to lift. Like when Alice shows him how to play handy-dandy.

"Watch," Alice says. She holds out her fists in front of Katherine.

"Handy dandy, prickly pandy, which hand will you have?"

Katherine chooses the left hand and finds a pretty red berry inside it. She giggles and tries to take the berry.

"Let's play again," Alice says, snatching her hands away and hiding them behind her back. "Handy dandy, prickly pandy, which hand will you have?"

Katherine chooses left again and gets an empty hand. Predictably, she pouts and fusses. Alice wags her finger at her, and I hear my words from years ago. "Katherine, it's a game. Sometimes you get the prize, sometimes you get the empty hand, but it's supposed to be fun every time."

Katherine tries hard to put on a happy face. "Fun," she says.

Then both girls play the game with Choupouke, and he is kept busy choosing hands. But when the game is over, his serious mood comes back. My hope is that little by little, Choupouke's sadness over Nemattanew's death will lift and he will be his happy self again.

• • •

March is time to plant peas, onions, and radishes, and this year we are planting on our own land. Our barn is ready for a cow, a mule, and chickens. Fields are cleared and ready to plant tobacco. My parents think it is too early to announce it, but I know that I will soon have another baby sister.

The trees are still bare but there is warmth in the air. Birds begin to return from their flight south to sing for us, and the first green shoots push up from the ground. I feel the hope of this new year.

On a beautiful Friday morning, I awake before dawn. I tiptoe past my sleeping family and walk outside. There is a light breeze and the air echoes with the chirping of spring peepers. I decide to start my chores early.

I lift the yoke and buckets to my shoulders and head toward the river. The sky has a glow in the east, but it is more the waning quarter moon that lights my path.

I am humming as I approach the barn where Choupouke sleeps. As I get closer, I stop my humming so I won't wake him. But I hear a strange noise. It is Choupouke's voice, making a tight, strangled sound. I run to the barn door and push it open. Choupouke is on his knees, his head hanging into his hands. He is swaying and groaning as if he is in great pain. I run to him.

"Choupouke, what is it? What has happened?" I cry.

He looks up. His cheeks are streaked with tears. He blinks at me as if he is not sure of what he is seeing in the dim light of the barn.

"Are you hurt?" I ask. I see no blood, no cuts or wounds.

There is torment in Choupouke's eyes. He reaches out to touch my face, but I instinctively push his hand away. The moment my hand touches his, I see it.

They come to help us work in the fields, with shovels and hoes, to help build houses, with hammers and saws, or to help fell trees with axes and wedges. They come to eat breakfast, and I see the colony's women slicing bread with kitchen knives. They come to each of the plantations and towns and farms, spreading out among the colonists like a spider's web being woven. It is like any other day; the natives coming to work and eat and live among us. But suddenly it all changes. Each of the natives grasps something nearby: a shovel, an ax, a kitchen knife, a hoe, a hammer. The next instant there is blood everywhere, as the hammers and shovels and axes come down on whoever is closest, women, children of all ages, men. No one has a chance to fight back. There is no warning.

I gasp. Choupouke is shaking. He is looking at me with such anguish that I know this vision must be true.

"When?" I demand.

He hangs his head back into his hands and starts up his moaning again. Of course, he won't answer me—how could he know that I know?

I pounce on him, shove him onto his back, and sit down hard on his chest. Before he can even react, I press my thumbs into his throat and shake him.

"When?" I screech. "When is the attack planned to happen?"

He looks shocked. "Today," he croaks out, his throat squeezed under my thumbs. "Morning."

I jump up and run. I am crying, tripping over roots. I fall down hard, gash my hand open on a sharp rock, but I am up again, running despite the pain.

I burst into our house. Mum is stoking the fire and the others are still sleeping. I am breathing too hard to speak. Mum sees my terror, the blood dripping from my hand.

"Virginia—" she whispers.

"Warning," I say between gasps for air. "Warning.

Everyone. Muskets. Swords. Cannons. *Stop them.*" I want to say, *Kill them*, but I remember what I felt from Choupouke when I had my thumbs against his throat: relief. They don't want to do this. They have been ordered to do it, and anyone who refuses will die the slow, tortured death of a traitor.

My breath slows down and I am able to speak. "Stop the natives. Don't let them come today. We must turn them around with our muskets and swords. Send them back home. Stop the attack before it starts."

Da and Samuel are awake and have heard me. Samuel is already on his way out the door. "I will go directly to Captain Newce," he says. "We will get the word out."

"How do you know this?" Da demands. "What—"

Mum interrupts him, "There is no time, John. She can tell you later."

Da is putting on his boots. "I will warn our neighbors," he says. He takes his sword down off the wall and gives it to Mum. Then he lights the fuse on his musket with a piece of kindling from the fire and carries his musket with him out the door.

"I want to go with Da," Alice says.

"Me too," Katherine says.

"You two just sit while I bandage your sister's hand," Mum says.

"No, Mum, there's no time," I say. "What about James Town?" Then suddenly a thought strikes me and I feel faint. "What about Martin's Hundred? I have to go! I have to tell them."

I start toward the door, but Mum grasps my arm. "Virginia, your hand is bleeding," she says firmly. "You cannot go."

The dizziness overtakes me and I begin to slump. Mum guides me to a chair. I sink down and rest my head in my good hand. When I close my eyes, I see the scene again, of violence and murder. I see Bermuda, his hands raised above his head the way he used to when Vincenzo beat him. I open my eyes to stop it.

Mum brings a bowl of hot water and begins to bathe my gashed hand. "You will have to trust God with James Town and Martin's Hundred and all the rest of the colony," she says gently. "Let Samuel and your father get the word out."

She presses cobwebs on my wound, and the sticky silk helps to knit the jagged edges of skin together. Then she bandages it with clean rags. Blood quickly soaks through the rags. Mum is right. I would never be able to paddle a canoe against the current. I would pass out from blood loss before I got even close to the other settlements.

I sit at the table as Mum dishes out porridge for the girls. She doesn't even expect me to eat.

Through our window I see Choupouke trudging up the hill to our house. It is what he does every morning to join us for breakfast before starting work with Da and

Samuel. But today it is as if he has leaden weights on his feet. *He is still fulfilling his orders*, I realize. I pick up Da's sword and stand in the doorway brandishing it.

"Go," I shout at Choupouke before he can get close. "Go away from us or I will slit your throat."

He is unarmed. Just like all the Indians I saw in the vision, he carries no weapon. *He will have to use our kitchen knife or Da's sword to kill me and Mum and my sisters.*

Choupouke stops and looks at me. He closes his eyes for a moment as though he is praying. Then he turns and walks off toward the forest.

Mum is right. I will have to trust God with the other towns and plantations. I will stay home to protect my sisters and my mother.

Forty-Five

DA AND SAMUEL return home in the afternoon. They say word got out to all of Elizabeth City. When the Indians began arriving to join the colonists for breakfast and work, or bringing meat and corn to trade, they were met with muskets and swords and axes. They were turned away before they could enter houses or pick up tools. There has been no attack on Elizabeth City today.

Samuel looks around. "Where's Choupouke?" he asks.

"Virginia says she is going to slit his throat," Alice says. "So, he left."

Samuel glances from Alice to me. "You said that?" he asks.

"He's an Indian, too, you know," I say. "It's not as if he had the choice to disobey orders just because he has been your friend forever."

"Is that who told you about the attack?" Da asks.

I hesitate a moment. Choupouke didn't become a traitor on purpose. And if I say he did, it could well mean his death at the hands of his own people. But I can't tell Da about the second sight, and I certainly don't want to start up witchcraft accusations here in our new home. "Yes, Choupouke told me," I say. I have spoken the truth. He told me with his touch.

◆ ◆ ◆

The sky has fallen. We don't dare travel, but messengers come to us. They come to report on the dead, and to count our dead, of which we have none. Three hundred and forty-seven men, women, and children, almost a quarter of the colony's population, were massacred in one day.

Captain Newce comes to check on us and to thank us for the warning that saved our settlement and the settlements closest to us. He was able to get the warning to Newport News as well.

"What about James Town?" Samuel asks warily. "How many dead there?"

Captain Newce brightens for a moment. "An Indian youth, a boy who lives with Richard Pace at Pace's Paines, told him about the planned attack. Mr. Pace rowed across the river to warn those at James Town fort and the glass house. In James Town they turned away the attackers at the fort gates. There were no casualties at any of those places."

"Thanks be to God," Mum says.

Samuel closes his eyes and lets out a shaky breath. Angela is safe.

"What about Martin's Hundred?" I ask.

Captain Newce shakes his head. "Martin's Hundred was one of the worst hit. Almost everyone is dead."

• • •

I sit on a rock near the river, looking out at the water, thinking, remembering. I think of Bermuda, streaks of clay on his face, arms outstretched, doing the celebration dance the day the glass house was almost ready.

I hear footsteps behind me and turn to see Samuel. He folds his lanky legs and sits beside me. We are silent for a while, with only the swish of the river current and birdsongs.

Samuel reaches into a pocket, then holds his two fists out for me to choose one. I touch his right hand, and when he opens it, I see the perfect skipping rock I'd given him for Bermuda. My eyes fill with tears.

"Did we get the empty hand this time?" I ask.

Samuel looks out at the river. "Isn't that the way it always is in life? Depending on how you see it, you always get the empty hand. And if you look at it another way, you always get the prize."

I hear my own voice in my head. *But it's supposed to be fun every time.*

"I'm not having fun right now," I say.

"But you will," Samuel says. "We will laugh again and be joyful again. You still have your sisters and mother and father." He touches my chin and turns my face toward him. "And you have *me*."

I blink and tears run down my cheeks. He puts his arm around me and I lean against him. The river swishes by and the birds sing.

          ◆ ◆ ◆

Over the next few weeks, we receive more news about the state of the colony. The plantations and outposts have all been abandoned. The surviving colonists have moved back to James Town and the more central settlements. They are in shock. They are terrified for their lives. And they are angry. Men have begun to organize retaliatory raids against Indian villages, killing and burning. We are at war.

We receive one piece of news that makes me feel that the whole world has gone mad: Our military men, especially the high-ranking ones, are admiring Chief Opechancanough's military strategy. They say he was brilliant the way he planned the attack and bided his time, waiting for us to become completely comfortable with his tribesmen living and working among us. They are impressed with the chief's military skills and hold him in high regard. War, and skill in war, is fascinating to them.

One day, Samuel and I are working together to plant

potatoes in our garden plot. Samuel digs a trench with the hoe, and I follow him, dropping seed potatoes with their long, ghostly sprouts into the trench.

"Do you think Chief Opechancanough will get what he wants?" I ask Samuel. "Do you think people will clamor to leave on the ships that come this spring and he will be rid of us?"

Samuel shakes his head. "They can clamor all they want. If they are still under contract to the Virginia Company of London, they have to stay."

I look out at the land we have cleared, where tiny tobacco plants are sprouting. I look at our garden plot with turnip seedlings, peas reaching up their trellis, and dark green onion tips sticking through the ground. "Do you think we will leave?" I ask in a small voice. "Mum's and Da's contracts are long over."

Samuel leans on his hoe a moment. "With you around to tell us whenever someone is going to try to kill us? No, I think we'll stay."

I give him a weak smile, but then my face drops again. "Maybe the prophecy can't be stopped," I say. "This is our third war with the natives." I remember the words I have recited so many times: *The third battle will be long and filled with bloodshed.* My throat tightens. "If this is the third battle from the prophecy, we will be at war for a long time."

Samuel cuts at the soil with his hoe, deepening his

trench. "And if the prophecy is true, then Chief Ope-chancanough will not get what he wants at all. Instead, this will be the end of his kingdom."

By the end of this battle, the Powhatan kingdom will be no more.

I shake my head. I think of Samuel's stories about when he lived with the Warraskoyacks, how he played ball games with the other boys. He had his hair shaved on one side and long on the other, so that his hair would not get in the way when he shot his bow and arrow. He says he looked more native than English in those days. I remember how he sat on reed mats with Captain Smith and Pocahontas and watched an exciting performance of dance and music by young tribal women, and feasted with the tribe afterward. I think of Pocahontas and her husband and young son in the Patawomeck village. I think of Nemattanew, with his magical wings. I remember Sarah, and her baby, and Pipsco and his little sister. I think of Choupouke, how he obviously did not want to carry out his part in the massacre. How could the vast Powhatan kingdom *be no more?*

"I wish we could have stayed at peace," I say.

• • •

Sadness wraps around me like a cloak. In late April, on Good Friday, I steal away to sit near the river by myself. Mum lets me go, leaving some of my work undone.

The sound of the water swishing by is comforting. The river has not changed just because the people who live along it are at war. In two days it will be Easter. We will go to church and Reverend Stockton will speak of the Resurrection and of hope. I shut my eyes and listen to the river. Where can I find hope?

I think of Pocahontas, how she lost so much and yet she found joy with her son Thomas and her adventure in England in the short time she had left to live. I think of Angela, how she has opened her heart to love with Samuel, even after all the love she has lost. With my eyes still closed, I remember my time imprisoned under the storehouse, before my trial, when I thought I might soon be hanged. I remember finding the light inside me that nothing could take away.

The sun shifts from behind a cloud and suddenly there is light full on my face. I smile. "That light is still there," I whisper to myself. "It is the light of my soul. It gives me the strength to be exactly who God created me to be."

"Virginia, is that you?" someone shouts from up the river.

I stand and shield my eyes from the sun. Coming toward me on the current is a rowboat laden with barrels and crates, with one man rowing and one woman passenger. The moment I recognize them, I shout, "Yes, it is me!" Then I run up the hill toward our cottage.

"Mum, come quickly!" I cry. "Look who is here!"

At the water's edge, Mum and Jane fall into each other's arms. Then Mum pulls back to take a good look at Jane. She is with child. Mum touches her belly gently. "I will help you when your time comes," she promises.

Robert lifts a crate from the rowboat. "I knew it would be good to get these two friends together," he says.

Da and Samuel join us and they help Robert unload the boat. They have brought their belongings and are moving to Elizabeth City. They will be living with Anthony Bonall and his family.

"So many survivors of the massacre have moved to James Town," Jane says. "They are grieving and fearful and angry. All they want is more war. They talk all day about revenge and more killing."

"We hoped it would be better here," says Robert.

"It is," says Mum. "We were spared." She looks at me proudly.

"I have a present for you, Virginia," Jane says. She pulls a bundle of rags out of her apron pocket and unwraps them. Inside is a small green drinking glass, slightly lopsided but definitely usable. "Bermuda wanted you to see how his skills improved."

I stare at the glass. My conversation with Captain Newce echoes in my head. *What about Martin's Hundred? . . . One of the worst hit. Almost everyone is dead.* "I'm glad—" I begin. I want to say, *I'm glad he had a chance to make glass before he died, since it was his dream.* But my words catch in my throat. I bite the inside of my mouth, willing myself not to cry here in front of everyone.

"Bermuda also sent you a message," Jane says. "That it is too hard for him to get away but he would love for you to come with Samuel next time he comes to James Town."

My mouth drops open.

"Of course, I'll bring her," Samuel says.

"It would cheer him up," says Robert. "He had just left Martin's Hundred and returned to the glass house a few days before the massacre. His parents knew how much he missed it and sent him back. His mum and da were both killed, and it has been hard for him."

"We will go soon," says Samuel.

"Yes," I say, finally finding my words. "Very soon."

"Virginia, come help me lay the table," Mum says. "We will eat and then get Jane and Robert settled."

Soon our house is loud with the voices of friends and family, and steamy from the boiling pot of venison stew. Jane bounces Katherine on her knees, making her laugh with a silly song about turnips. Mum slices fresh bread, I ladle up the bowls, and Alice places our new deer-skull spoons around the table. Da, Samuel, and Robert talk about the crop of tobacco that is sprouting nicely.

As I look around the room, I realize that Samuel is right. I have love, and that is the prize.

Forty-Six

———

I HAVE A dream of ships.

First, they are the ships I know, sailing to shore on the wind with white billowed sails. But then they become huge, sleek ships with wings like birds, sailing high above the earth, pushed by an unseen hand.

The ships carry children, so many of them. They are not the sad children who come to James Town against their will. These children are joyful and excited about this journey to the New World. They know peace inside themselves and so they bring peace to this land. They come here from every corner of the world, with skin of different hues, speaking languages that mix like the notes of music.

They bring a message to all the old ones: the time for fighting is over. The time for life in joy together is here.

When I wake, it feels as though I have dreamed far into the future—too far for this good news to be mine. But it will belong to someone, sometime. And this gives me hope.

—*Virginia Laydon, the hungry month of April 1622*

Author's Note

I AM OFTEN asked how much of a book is real and how much is from my imagination. In *Poison in the Colony* I have recounted the most significant events of those years as faithfully as I could, relying on historical records and accounts that were written by the people who were there. The story is a combination of what really did happen and what could have happened. Each character in the book either was a real person or, in the case of some of the minor characters such as Cecily or William, bears the name of a real person taken from the records. There is one exception to this: Leone, the Italian glassmaker who was kind and helpful to Bermuda. I had no records for him and so I named him after my Italian grandfather.

This book is similar to *Blood on the River* in that, as I had to do with Samuel Collier, I had to invent a personality and characteristics for my main character, Virginia Laydon. As I pondered who Virginia was and what she would be like, I began to get a clear picture of her as someone with the gift, or curse, of what was called in those days the second sight. In modern times it might well be called having a strong intuitive sense. Virginia calls it "the knowing" because that is how she experiences it and she has no other reference for it. My inspiration for this trait in Virginia came from a good friend of mine who is both extremely intuitive and a descendent of the first Jamestown settlers. Her ancestor plays a bit part in the story. I knew from talking to my friend that this gift has caused grief and danger in her own life and in the lives of her forebearers who also had this ability. She remains steadfast in the knowledge that the gift is from God and is to be used in service to Him *only*. In the days of witch hunts, this ability was often misunderstood, sometimes misused, and would no doubt have been a potentially lethal liability.

It was only after I had decided upon Virginia having this trait that I discovered some very interesting facts about events in Jamestown. Virginia's mother, along with Jane Wright (sometimes written Joan or Joane), the left-handed midwife, were assigned to make shirts for the colonists and given bad thread. They were thus framed for the crime of stealing thread from the colony, tried by Governor Dale, pronounced guilty, and brutally whipped. Ann Laydon miscarried the child she was carrying.

Why were they framed? Being left-handed was often seen as witchlike. And being a midwife and a healer with herbs, as many midwives were, was also seen as possible witch behavior. Having a bad outcome for a patient with a birth or an illness could bring on the accusations.

Then I discovered that Jane Wright was the first person to be formally accused of witchcraft in the Virginia colony, in September 1626. Something was telling me I was on the right track with giving Virginia this special ability. The testimony given by Charles during Virginia's trial is taken from the actual testimony during a later witch trial in the Virginia colony, that of Grace Sherwood. Yes, a woman actually said that Grace Sherwood came into her room at night, sat on her, then went out through the keyhole as a black cat!

Poison in the Colony covers the true historical events that occurred during those years, though Virginia's part in them is of my own invention. All we really know about Virginia Laydon is that she was the first English child born in Jamestown, she and her family lived in Jamestown, then her parents were given land in Elizabeth City, and the family moved there to their own farm. They thrived and survived and were still there with Virginia and her three younger sisters, Alice, Katherine, and baby Margaret, for the census of 1624.

What about Bermuda? He was born on the island of Bermuda, to Mr. and Mrs. Eason, but after that I cannot find him. So for him, too, I had to make up his personality and desires. Did he dream of making glass and become a glassmaker when the glass house was started up again? We will never know. But the events around the glass house—when it was started, when it was abandoned and then started up again with the Italian glassworkers—are all accurate. Vincenzo was a real person and was as violent as I have depicted him. His wife was sent back to Italy because the governor feared Vincenzo would kill her, and he did take a crowbar to the big furnace and break it after the men had worked for weeks to repair it.

The true parts of Angela's story are that she was brought

to Jamestown on the *Treasurer* as a stolen slave and was either sold or escaped from the ship. It is also true that she was sent to live as a servant for Captain and Mrs. Pierce, who paid her purchase price. Sometimes her name is printed in the records as "Angelo," but this is incorrect because that is the male form of the name. Anansi tales are believed to have originated in Ghana, and were known from Senegal to Ndongo (located in present-day Angola), where Angela was from.

For the character of Charles, I simply took his name from the census records and gave him that nasty personality. (Apologies to the real Charles.) Choupouke was an Indian youth who lived with the colonists. I do not know if he ever worked or stayed with Virginia and her family, but he was living in Elizabeth City with the colonists after the massacre, in 1624.

What of the controversy about how Pocahontas died? The English version of the events has always been that she fell ill from a common disease such as tuberculosis and perished. However, in 2007, Dr. Linwood "Little Bear" Custalow and Angela L. Daniel "Silver Star," representatives of the Mattaponi tribe in Virginia, published *The True Story of Pocahontas: The Other Side of History* (Fulcrum Publishing). In this book, they share the sacred Mattaponi oral history that has been handed down through the generations, beginning with Pocahontas's sister Mattachanna and her husband, Uttamattamakin (Tomocomo), who were with Pocahontas the night she died. The sacred history says that she was fine and healthy when she went to have dinner with her husband, John Rolfe, and

Captain Argall. After dinner, she came to her room and was suddenly ill, vomiting and convulsing, and soon died. It looked very much as though she had been poisoned at dinner. As with so many things in history, we will never know for sure what actually happened.

Mr. George Thorpe really did hang two dogs after natives said they were afraid of them. He was trying very hard to convince the natives to send their children to his school, and somehow thought this would help his cause. The natives were quite insulted by his constant attempts at reeducating their children. When he was killed in the massacre, they treated his body with the contempt reserved for enemies to show their displeasure with him.

Nemattanew was a warrior who wore feathers and swan's wings on his arms and who was seen as magical and immortal by his people. He had been in many battles and never been injured, and so his fellow warriors believed that English muskets could not affect him. The colonists nicknamed him Jack of the Feather and did not respect him nearly as much as his people did. It is also sadly true that when Nemattanew came back from his trading trip with Mr. Morgan, wearing Mr. Morgan's cap and unable to explain what happened because of the language barrier, he was indeed shot by the English muskets. As he died, he begged, with his few English words, to be buried in Jamestown so that his people would not find out that he could be killed by a musket after all. Many historians believe that the killing of Nemattanew was pivotal in Chief

Opechancanough's decision to move forward with his plan for the March massacre.

Sometimes it has been reported incorrectly that the 1622 massacre happened on Good Friday. This is why I have shown in the story that Easter came weeks after that fateful day. Dates and calendars that far back can be confusing. The colonists were still going by the Julian calendar, and so for them, New Year's Day was March 25, which means that the attack actually happened on March 22, 1621. Since our modern calendar has New Year's Day falling on January 1, the date is officially reported as March 22, 1622. There was another massacre years later, on April 18, 1644, that occurred on Maundy Thursday, the Thursday before Easter. It is interesting to note that in both 1622 and 1644, the attacks happened one day shy of the third quarter moon. That is the moon that lit Virginia's way as she walked past the barn and heard Choupouke's anguish that morning.

For primary source material about the prophecy that was given to Chief Powhatan by his high priests (pages 47–49), see William Strachey, *The History of Travel into Virginia Britannia: The First Book of the First Decade, 1612*, reprinted in Edward Wright Haile, ed., *Jamestown Narratives: Eyewitness Accounts of the Virginia Colony: The First Decade: 1607–1617*. Champlain, Virginia: RoundHouse, 1998, pages 662–63; and Uttamatomakkin (Tomocomo), "An Interview in London," reprinted in *Jamestown Narratives*, p. 881.

A word about music and dance: Jamestown was the site of

the first mixing of musical traditions from Europe, Africa, and North America. Music and dance are languages that all can speak. The combining of rhythms, instruments, and dance steps from these three distinct areas of the world has resulted in some of the forms we now know as traditional American music and dance. For example, the banjo was born of West African stringed instruments and the fiddle has a long tradition in Europe. These two instruments come together in American old-time string band music. Traditional dance from Ndongo, Algonquian traditional dance, and Irish step dancing were first introduced to each other during the music jams in Jamestown. Many dance historians believe that African, Native American, and British traditions later combined to create the quiet upper body, toe- and heel-tapping, high-stepping moves of Appalachian clogging. As both a musician and a dancer, it was fascinating to write about these jam sessions in early Jamestown and imagine that first coming-together of this melting pot of music and dance. Try this: watch clips of each of these types of dance and see if you can discern which elements of each became incorporated into traditional Appalachian clogging!

There are several ways to continue to experience what it was like in the Virginia colony during the early 1600s. Jamestown Settlement is where you will find the ships, cottages, muskets, an Indian village, reenactors, and even chickens all working together to bring those early years of the settlement to life. To see the archeological dig, artifacts, and parts of the original Jamestown church, visit Historic Jamestowne. There are also descendants of the Powhatan empire still living in Virginia. There are tribal museums to explore and powwow celebrations that are open to the public, with drumming, singing, dancing, and other traditional arts.

For more information about visiting Jamestown or to find out more about its history online, go to historyisfun.org/jamestown-settlement, historicjamestowne.org, and virginia.org/virginiaindians. Your time travel experience awaits!

Acknowledgments

I WOULD LIKE to thank the many fourth and fifth graders who wrote me letters to tell me how much they wanted a sequel to *Blood on the River: James Town 1607*. This book is for you!

I would also like to thank my editor, Tracy Gates, for her belief in me and in this book, and for always knowing what my stories need to make them better. Many thanks to Nancy Brennan for designing the book so beautifully, to Bagram Ibatoulline for the gorgeous cover, and to the careful copy editors who do so much to help keep details accurate: Janet Pascal, Abigail Powers, Krista Ahlberg, Marinda Valenti, Laura Stiers, and Kaitlin Severini.

For my research I depended heavily upon some of the same sources I used in *Blood on the River*. I pored over the first person accounts written by the colonists themselves. I went back to my notes from interviews with historians at Historic Jamestowne and from powwows held by several Virginia Indian tribes.

Then there were the new things I needed to learn about, such as what it feels like to shoot one's first deer, what it's like to be highly intuitive, what you would do with a live fish in a canoe. These days, the internet can answer many questions, but I still find interviews to be an invaluable source. And so I would like to thank my willing interviewees: Nancy Doran of the Maryland Department of Natural Resources; Cynthia Sexton; Brigid Hopkins; Laurie Little; Shannon Warren; and the many reenactors at the Jamestown Settlement and Powhatan Indian Village.

While this is a work of fiction, I have strived to make this book as accurate and true to life as possible. Any inaccuracies it still contains are entirely my own.